MR. TILLING'S BASEMENT

& OTHER STORIES

EDWARD LEE

deadite press

DEADITE PRESS
833 SE Main Street #342
Portland, OR 97214
www.DEADITEPRESS.com

An imprint of Eraserhead Press
www.eraserheadpress.com

ISBN: 978-1-62105-325-5

ACKNOWLEDGMENTS

Christine Morgan, Rose O'Keefe, John Baltisberger, K. Trap Jones, Dave Wilson, Roman, Gary Hguonodcm, Hector Fonseca, Brandon Thompson, Craig M. Steele, Peggy Howes, Gordon Jones, Dustin LaValley, Daniel Volpe, Tommy865, Chris Newton, Artur Kouri, Voracious Gnome, John Petitt, James Flynn, Phobophile, The Book Dweller, somegorilla, Lydia Peever, Jessica Hause.

CONTENTS

MR. TILLING'S
BASEMENT

Built in the '50s, six hundred square feet, with a yard like a prairie, it was not exactly a show piece, but it was more than a sensible, modest retiree like Tilling would ever need. The kind of house Tilling's dear dead father would've called "Craptastic." The place was the just the right price: dirt cheap. *Oh, well,* he thought, looking in the chipped mirror that hung in the stripped cubby-sized bedroom. *Old, bald, bad knees, and this is the end of the rainbow.*

But Tilling was a "glass half-empty" kind of guy and at least he knew it. It really wasn't that bad, and not owning a car left extra money for the finer things in life, like Amazon Prime and sushi from UberEats a few times a week.

The bathroom had a shower the size of a telephone booth—if such things still existed—a utility room not much bigger, and then the rest, which was just one big room that served as kitchen and living room together. New interior paint was in order because the eyesore gold-flecked white paint had by now turned tan, with lighter squares all over the place from former framed pictures and furniture. But Tilling actually doubted he would ever undertake the task. *Why bother? I don't give a shit, and I don't think Better Homes and Gardens will be coming to do a shoot anytime soon.*

What little of his furniture he'd decided to keep was haphazardly arranged: a shitty old couch, a threadbare armchair, and a warped coffee table. In a broom closet next to the basement door stood a chest of fake mahogany drawers festooned with cobwebs, a remnant from the previous owner, of which Tilling knew almost nothing. The place had been on the market for a year until the economy upticked, but the price had gone down, which seemed odd. At first he wondered if he'd bought a "stigmatized" house, but the real-estate agent, if she could be believed in this day and age, had assured him that no one had ever died here, no murders, no violent crimes, and no kidnapped women had been caged in the basement. And that reminded him—

The basement...

He'd only taken a peek at it when the real-estate agent first showed him the house. It seemed to exist under the same footprint of the house but wasn't counted in the square footage: just a drab, mildewy basement with a cement floor, an ancient hot-water heater, and an equally ancient fusebox, the kind with the old screw-in fuses. Tilling went down now, which took twice as long as a normal person, due to what the doctor called his "medial meniscus tear." Did he want a knee replacement? *Hell no.*

Little eye-level windows that showed the outside at ground-level ringed the perimeter. The old hot-water heater ticked. He wouldn't be storing anything down here because his knee would hurt too damn much going up and down. That ubiquitous mildew smell permeated everything, that and something faint like old woodsmoke, or was it incense? In one corner stood a man-high storage thing made of two-by-fours and surrounded by chicken wire. Inside, some rakes, brooms, and garden tools leaned, plus some boxes labeled STUFF, JUNK, and XMAS in magic marker. There was also a battery powered weed-whacker. *Wow. Is it possible for a basement to be LESS interesting?* he thought, then limped back upstairs.

One thing he couldn't get rid of were his boxes of textbooks— some which he had written himself in days gone by—from his college office. Here they were, piled up in the corner of the living room by the TV. He knew he was fooling himself when he thought, *I'll have to hire someone to lug all that down to the basement,* because the truth was the boxes would likely remain where they sat until the day he died. Tilling was a loner, something of a scholarly recluse so, no, he wouldn't paint over the white squares on the walls, nor would he paper, nor would he replace the carpets which clearly had been installed when the house was built, probably when Eisenhower was in office. Tilling was not disconsolate at all over the probability that his front door would never be disturbed by the knock of a visitor—

And at that precise moment, someone knocked on his front door.

Damn them! I JUST put up the No Soliciting sign!

When he opened the door and said, rather uncongenially, "Yes?" he was taken aback. The knocker proved to be an attractive young woman, perhaps in her mid- to late-'20s, with long shiny black hair, tight frayed jeans, and a blouse that contained what, in his younger and more sexist days, he would've referred to as a "motherlode of boob." She had dark, razor-sharp eyes and a light tea-colored complexion; that and a hemp collar ridged by what he thought were lava-stone beads led him to an immediate guess that she was Native American.

"Hi, my name's Tevi," she said, in a tone of voice that seemed full of vigor and enthusiasm. "I don't mean to bother you but I was wondering—"

"Look, I don't mean to sound rude," Tilling began, "but if you're selling something, I can assure you that I'm not the least bit—"

She grinned. "Only thing I'm selling is knowledge."

The confident way she'd said that made Tilling give her the benefit of the doubt. "Knowledge, huh? You might say I recently retired from a *career* of selling knowledge, so, young lady...you've secured my attention."

"Great. I was just wondering if you know Jerry, or were friends with him in any way, because if not—"

"I don't know anyone named Jerry."

"Well, his real name is Jeronymous, if you can fuckin' believe that. It was too much of a mouthful so he just told everyone to call him Jerry. Jerry Orne. The guy who used to own this house."

Tilling was trying hard not to stare at her bosom, which was clearly devoid of a bra beneath a simple powder-blue blouse. "Oh, I see. Well, no, I never knew him. The real-estate agent said he was in his '80s, I think."

"Early '90s, actually," Tevi said. "He's really something. Sharp as a tack till recently, and, well, never mind."

"Did I understand the real-estate agent right? Mr. Orne is still alive?"

"Jerry, yeah, he's still alive, all right. At first I would visit him every now and then. But eventually there was no point."

Tilling nodded, suspecting something like Alzheimer's. "I see. The agent indicated he was in a nursing home."

"Yeah, a place called Serenity Towers, but most people call it *Senility* Towers. It's a high end memory care facility. Costs a fuckin' fortune."

Tilling figured that Orne must have top-notch nursing care insurance. And perhaps he might want to look into that himself sometime.

"First his mind went—dementia, you know? So he stopped knowing who I was, so I stopped going. I think it just confused him more. And a little later he had a bunch of strokes, so he's pretty much a vegetable. Can't talk, can't move, has to be spoon-fed. Like that."

"Quite a grim consequence. I'm sorry to hear it. I only hope he had a full life."

"Oh, he did, that's for sure. Like you wouldn't believe."

Tilling was finding this interesting but he was letting it drift off track. "So, Tevi. Tell me about this *knowledge* that you're selling."

"I guarantee you, it's info you'll be interested in."

"And how much will this info lighten a retiree's wallet?"

Here came her beaming smile again. "Only thirty bucks!"

"Mmmm," Tilling murmured, eyes narrowed. "I don't think so."

"Well, okay," she said. "Have a nice day. I hope you enjoy your new house." And then she turned and began to walk away.

Once a sucker, always a sucker, Tilling told himself. "Okay, Tevi. Thirty dollars."

She turned and bopped back up. "Great! Let's go! Down to the basement—"

* * * *

He had to practically hop back down the stairs due to his knee, while she buzzed right down. Once he made it down himself, he found the mildew smell possibly even stronger.

"Wow," Tevi said. "I can still smell it, even after all this time."

"The mildew, yes—"

"No, not that. That smoky, bitter scent. Can you smell it?"

Tilling nodded. "And even upstairs too a little, like woodsmoke but there's no fireplace. Do you know if there was ever a fire in the house?"

"There was no fire," she said, walking toward the chicken-wire cage. "It's jimsonweed and lophop but also some other things he never told me."

Interesting, Tilling thought. He knew what jimsonweed and lophophora cactus were, but he thought it best to keep that to himself for now. *Let her keep talking...* He'd always believed it smarter to talk less and listen more, especially when encountering a stranger.

"Do you notice anything weird down here?" she asked. Now she was bending over to fiddle with the latch on the chicken-wire closet, and Tilling couldn't help but notice her elucidated butt and the braless breasts swaying in the blouse. *Damn it,* he thought. *This girl's got some body going on...* "Weird? Um, other than the smell, no, I don't think so."

She stood back up straight and faced him. There was just something about her attitude and expression that seemed lively, enthused; Tilling found it impossible not to like her in spite of the fact that he knew virtually nothing about her. *I just let a perfect stranger not only into my house but into my basement. She could pull a gun me, rob me and kill me, and no one would even hear the shot.* But this, Tilling knew, was his darker, pessimistic self kicking in. *Maybe she's casing the joint so some big lummox ex-con boyfriend can sneak back in tonight while the feeble old man sleeps and then clean me out.* And at this he nearly laughed out loud. *There's nothing to clean out except a twenty-year-old tube television and a ten-year-old microwave.*

"What's so funny?" she asked, noticing that he was smiling for no ostensible reason.

"Nothing, just me. I'm sorry, what were you saying? Oh, no, I'm not really noticing anything weird down here."

"Doesn't this basement look smaller than the upstairs of the house?"

Tilling glanced around, then paused. "Well, now that you mention it, yes, I suppose it does." Next, a longer pause—it was not simply the power of suggestion—and a raised brow. "You're not going to tell me there's a secret room down here, are you?"

She spun back around and entered the wire closet, and with some clatter, moved away the weed-whacker, the rakes and shovels, etc. and slid the storage boxes away from the back wall. "You won't believe this!" A sheet of high plywood formed the rear of the closet. Tevi removed it, revealing a doorway.

Tilling was astounded. "You're kidding me! There *is* a secret room!"

Tevi smiled and nodded. "That's not what Jerry called it, but... yeah. You're about to learn some cool stuff about the guy who used to live here." She took a flashlight hanging off a hook. "Ready?"

To say that Tilling was intrigued would be understatement. He bent over and followed the energetic woman into the black opening. There was a strange shift in temperature; it seemed warmer when he would've thought it should be cooler. Tevi roved the flashlight around, to disclose a cinderblock-lined room and cement floor covered by straw mats like the kind people would take to the beach. In here, that bitter smoke scent was more abundant. On the floor stood six candles in stands, and against the narrow side wall was one of those white plastic put-it-together-yourself shelf units, four shelves in all, loaded with jars and what appeared to be old cigar boxes. The bottom shelf contained some paperback books. The room itself looked about six feet by twenty.

"Wow," Tilling said. "And what is this place?"

Tevi glanced slowly around. Then, grinning, she looked wide-eyed at Tilling, as if she was pleased by his surprise. "Jerry called this place his 'chancel.'"

"Chancel? As in a *church* cancel?"

Her attention suddenly seemed diverted. "Sort of, I guess. Fuck... This brings back memories..."

Was she being cryptic on purpose? Tilling didn't think so. With the penlight on his own key ring, he examined the items on the set of shelves. Mason jars sat in rows, some containing dark liquids, some containing powdered substances or leafy materials of things like dried weeds and flowers. He touched the lid of an old King Edward cigar box. "Jerry, I take it, liked cigars, and bad ones at that."

"No, he didn't smoke," she said softly. "He just liked the boxes to store things in. They sell 'em at junk shops and garage sales."

Tilling flipped up the lid on the box and in it discovered several smoking pipes. He picked one up and found it surprisingly heavy; the bowl, he discerned now, was fashioned from carved stone. The inside was charred.

He held the pipe up. "So Jerry didn't smoke, huh?"

"I meant, he didn't smoke tobacco," she said but all of a sudden she seemed listless, snagged by some discomfiting reminder. It was as though her previous good spirits and enthused energy were a punctured balloon. "This place creeps me out. Let's go back upstairs, okay?" And before Tilling could answer, she was already out of the arcane room and trotting up the steps.

He felt like an old invalid straining back up the stairs, one step at a time. *I wonder what this is really all about? And this Jerry guy, Jerry Orne.* Once he got his computer hooked up he'd have to search the name.

'I'm hoping that my thirty dollars will furnish more information than that," Tilling said. He remained standing while he looked down at her as she sat on the ancient couch. "So...you and this Mr. Orne, I take it, would use that secret room—"

"The chancel," she sullenly corrected.

"Of course. The chancel. The two of you would go down there for the purpose of entertaining yourselves by way of psychedelic experience—"

"It wasn't entertainment," Tevi said, looking down. Her hands were clasped in her lap. "Don't make judgments when you don't understand."

Tilling nodded. "It's not a judgment by any means, it's an informed deduction. I happen to know that jimsonweed and lophophora are historically known to be rich in tropane alkaloids, compounds that occur in mescaline and pellotine, very similar to peyote."

He expected her to show some surprise in his knowledge of such things. "I don't know anything about fuckin' tropane-whatever-you-just-said, and it wasn't just jimson and lophop that Jerry used." She pointed to the broom closet by the basement door, which Tilling had already looked into but had not yet investigated with any scrutiny. "I already told you, Jerry put other ingredients in the mix but I got no idea what it was. It's in the books in that closet."

Hmm... Tilling opened the closet at once, used his knuckles to push aside nets of cobwebs that covered the cheap dresser, and opened the topmost drawer. Several very old books sat within; one was entitled *Murray's Guide to Sussex,* but when he opened it he found no such book, but instead a coverless tome whose title seemed to be *Liber Nigrae Peregrinationis.* Tilling guessed something like *The black book of travels or adventures?* Why had the real book been hidden within the cover of a more innocuous one? At any rate, there was no use trying to read any of it because he'd never mastered much Latin. *Well, I can read Cuneiform, Sumerian, and Greek but I don't suppose there's any of that here.* Here was another book, this one whole, in German—another language Tilling didn't know. *Some damn scholar I turned out to be.* It was by someone named Von Juntz, called, preposterously, *Unaussprechlichen Kulten,* which he could only guess meant "unspeakable cults." Several more, smaller books in Latin occupied this top shelf. "So I take it your friend Jerry was well versed in Latin and German."

"He was well versed in a lot of shit," Tevi said hollowly. "Look at the stuff in the second drawer. Tell me what language *that* is."

For some reason he couldn't identify, there was something exciting about this. Maybe it was because he was a morose retiree suddenly in the presence of an attractive young woman who was actually paying attention to him. But the contents of the second drawer brought any such further ponderings to an end. Several manila folders lay in the drawer, and on each one someone had scribbled in ballpoint *Pnakotic mms,* then *Glakki,* then *Alko.* Tilling was wholly unfamiliar with these words. Next, he opened the first folder and found it stuffed with typical eight and a half by eleven printer paper, but each sheet (photocopies, evidently) was filled with handwritten scrawl in no language Tilling had ever seen. The other folders were the same. *What the hell?* "These are xeroxes of hand-written copies of three separate languages that I can't identify."

Tevi wasn't at all surprised. "Jerry could read all that shit. He said one of 'em's half a million years old."

"That's impossible," Tilling snapped. "Language doesn't go back that far, and neither does the human race."

"Believe what you want. I guess you're not much for thinking outside the box."

Tilling frowned, looking at the sheaf bending in his hand. Throughout, passages had been highlighted. "Did Jerry make translations of any of this?"

"Nope." She pointed to her head. "He kept the translations up here. He was pretty smart. I could pick most any book off his shelf and say 'What's the first paragraph on page 108?' and nine times out of ten he'd get it right. He's fuckin' brilliant—er, was, before his mind crapped out."

Yeah, brilliant. I guess he was...and I guess I'm not...

She was still sitting there as if dejected. What had happened? "Is something wrong?" he asked, a bit hastily. "When you first came in here, you were bright-eyed and bushy-tailed and now, after one short trip to the basement? You're acting like you're clinically depressed."

"It's just—" she began but didn't finish.

"What, you and Jerry used to smoke hallucinogens in the basement and you had a—whatever they call it—a bad trip?"

"I only smoked the shit once. Jerry smoked it dozens of times, or maybe even hundreds. He'd pay me to sit with him—"

"*Sit* with him?" Tilling's frown sharpened; crow's feet at the corners of his eyes drew deeper, like the perfect agitated old man whose moribundity was now self-evident. "Come on, what are you talking about?"

Tevi exhaled as if inconvenienced. "Okay, I got to know Jerry one day when I was walking by the house. I was going door to door asking people if I could clean for them, or walk their dogs, or paint. Jerry was the only one who hired me. You've looked at your shitty yard, right? There's not enough grass to even bother buying a mower for so he ordered a weed-whacker and said he'd pay me twenty bucks to trim the grass. When the clumps get too high, the HOA will complain, so I'd take care of it. You might want to hire me too because—no offense—I can't really picture you swinging the weed-whacker when it's ninety degrees."

I can't either, he thought. "Tevi, do you know what 'convoluted' means?"

"I don't know—fucked up I think, like all over the place, right?"

"Right. You're convoluting the topic; your answer to my question is, indeed, all over the place and peppered with digressions. I didn't ask you about the weed-whacker or the yard or anything else except what you meant when you said he'd pay you to *sit* with him when he was smoking some psychedelic stuff down in the basement."

She rolled her eyes. "Shit, man, I'm just trying to give you some fuckin' background about how I got to know Jerry in the first place. He wound up hiring me for a bunch of stuff, vacuuming, cleaning the bathroom and kitchen, and, well, other stuff..."

Her verbal pause induced a mental pause for Tilling. "What other stuff?"

She shrugged. "Every Friday night he'd pay me fifty bucks to blow him, and he'd also get me whatever dinner I wanted from one of the delivery places. He was great. And you really gotta admire a guy who can pull a rock-hard boner when he's pushing ninety. I swear, you could flap it and it would bounce like a fuckin' diving board." She chuckled. "And he could come a lot too, none of that enlarged prostate shit with Jerry."

Tilling stood silent, his mouth hanging open.

"Well, you asked," she said.

"Yes, um, yes I did," Tilling replied. "It's just that I wasn't expecting an answer quite so richly detailed..."

"Just so you know, the offer stands for you too. If you were an asshole, I'd probably be able to tell by now. You seem all right."

More silence from Tilling, more subtle shock. *No diving board here, I'm afraid.* "Well, Tevi, I'll have to...give that some thought."

After her brazen confession, she seemed to be returning to her previous bubbly demeanor, and there was something lively and honest about her nonchalant profanity, where as, with anyone else it would feel trashy. He was about to ask, again, about the "sitting," but then she maintained her previous tangent, a rather autobiographical one. "I don't know what I would've done without Jerry—when I first met him I was *all* fucked up. Working the street, turning tricks, selling dope. I even did porn—jeez, what a hosebag, huh?"

This piqued Tilling's interest; he'd always been something of a voyeur. "Really? Genuine pornography?"

"Oh, sure," she dismissed. "Believe it or not, this is a big county for porn and B&D. Tevi's not a very common name; look it up on Clips for Sale, and my stuff should pop right up. I'm not proud of some of the shit I did but—fuck—a girl's gotta do what she's gotta do. I had a kid to feed, well, for awhile. Then the state took him, so the only thing I had left to feed after that was a pill habit. Beans, Roxies, you know." She got up briskly and went to the kitchen area. "But I beat it. When you hit rock bottom enough times, you either quit or die. So I said fuck it and quit. Say, do you still have any of that wine?"

Tilling was still trying to collate all of this information. "Wine?"

Tevi opened a cupboard and squealed delightedly. "Thank God, it's still here!" and then she took down a bottle of what appeared to be Manischewitz. Next she opened another cupboard and withdrew some paper cups.

"You really know your way around," Tilling said.

"Oh, sure. I spent tons of time here, but I wonder why the real-estate agent didn't take the wine. And don't worry, I'm not gonna go nuts with the *firewater*. You know how us 'Injuns' are." Tevi laughed. "I won't scalp you."

Tilling gestured to his bald head. "Not much to scalp here."

She was just about to fill her cup. "Oh, shit, I didn't even ask. You don't mind, do you?"

"Not at all, and don't bother offering me any because my doctor strongly advised me to eliminate all alcohol unless I want to assure myself of a premature death."

"Bummer," she said.

Tilling shook his head, amused. *Jerry could've at least picked up some higher quality vino. That stuff isn't exactly Chateau Lafite...*

She sat right up on the kitchen counter with her ankles crossed. "So, as I was saying—oh, by the way, Tevi is Hopi for dancer." She laughed. "Figures. I can't dance for shit."

"The Hopi Tribe? Arizona, correct?"

"Yep. How'd you know that?"

"I'm a teacher, a professor—er, used to be, for over three decades," Tilling replied, not at all impressed. "I've taught history and anthropology at several different colleges. And for a few years, I taught some classes on ancient Meso and Native American cultures. That's how I knew about jimsonweed and lophop—hallucinogenic precursors for summoning a vision quest."

"Cool," she said, sipping wine,

"So why did you leave Arizona and come here?"

"Are you kidding? It's a hundred and twenty degrees in the summer, here it's only ninety. And I needed to get far away from my ex. He was an asshole—well, *all* of them were. I sure know how to pick 'em, huh? But I got no one to blame but myself. The dudes with the biggest cocks are always the biggest shit-heads."

Tilling could not conceive of a response. "So. Back to what you were saying. Jerry paid you to *sit* with him, while he engaged in some sort of vision quest?"

She smiled as if he'd said something inept. "It's nothing like a vision quest. Jerry was an adventurous guy; he spent his whole life searching for mysteries almost no one knew anything about. It's from those photocopies you were looking at—shit that only he could read. You'd never know it by looking at this house, but Jerry was rich as fuck—"

This immediately bade more of Tilling's curiosity. "Really? What was his job? What did he do to earn money?"

She looked right at him with a dark smile. "He never told me. Inheritance, I guess, or old family money."

"But if he was so rich, what did he spend all his money on?"

Tevi finished her wine and was now leaning back on the counter, on her hands. This instigated something of a provocative pose: her legs spread almost lewdly, her braless breasts displayed at the perfect angle. Tilling wondered if she were doing this deliberately. "He traveled all over the world, for decades. Once he went all the way to Argentina just to go to a library—"

"The Biblioteca Nacional!" Tilling exclaimed. "It's very famous. I'd always wanted to go there myself but...never got around to it."

"Well, Jerry went to lots of libraries, fuckin' France, Germany, Egypt, Russia and countries I never heard of—just to read weird shit," she said. "He went to ancient castles in Europe, shrines on mountains in fuckin' China and Tibet. He went to the ruins of Babylon in Iraq or Iran or some shit. There was one place where he said he saw the ghost of a wizard or warlock or something—fuck, what was it called? Nina, er, no, ninuh something—"

Tilling was so riveted by what she was saying that he'd completely stopped noticing her body. "*Nineveh!* The lucky bastard. It was the capital of the Assyrian Empire over three thousand years ago, and the most powerful city on earth."

She was wagging her flip-flopped feet off the edge of the counter. "Yeah, see? You know about this shit." She gazed up at the ceiling as if forcing a recollection. "Jerry went to all kinds of off-the-wall places—he went to Stonehenge, he went to some battlefield in Germany where a hundred thousand guys got killed in one afternoo—"

"Probably Leipzig," Tilling supposed. "Napoleon's last battle—a slaughter."

"And he went to that island—Easter Island—with the big stone heads looking up at the sky. Oh, and what was the name of that other place—fuck? Yeah! He also went to Chorazin; I think it's in Israel. You know anything about Chorazin?"

21

"Indeed I do," Tilling said. "It's a ruin, and yet another place I'd always wanted to go to but never got around to it. Two millennia ago, it was a town on the Sea of Galilee and is referenced in the Bible as a town that Jesus Christ put a curse on."

"Right! Wow!" Tevi said excitedly. "You're a smart dude—"

"Thanks—"

"—almost as smart as Jerry."

Terrific, Tilling thought with a smirk. "Okay, so why did Jerry lavish huge sums of money to travel to famous historical locations around the globe?"

"I told you, for knowledge, to learn things he was interested in. His life's adventure," she replied. She poured herself more wine.

His life's adventure, Tilling glumly repeated the words. Tilling was a life-long academic with degrees from Harvard and Columbia. He doubted that this man Jerry was really smarter than him. But—

But—

Jerry's life was an extraordinary adventure in his thirst for knowledge, however bizarre that knowledge might be, Tilling calculated. *But what's MY life been? I spent the last thirty years teaching students things that people don't really even care about anymore. But Jerry? He traveled the word to actually SEE those things. He went out and DID it—*

Tilling stared off, feeling the edge of depression.

Yeah, he DID it. But all I ever did was read about it...

"Somebody shoot your dog?" she asked, clearly noting the sudden downswing of his mood.

"What? Oh, well...sometimes when people get old, they fall into the habit of thinking in reverse." Tilling was staring at nothing, but staring still. "You think back about all the things you never did when you had the chance..."

"Oh, you're not *that* old. Jerry was old as fuck but he had more energy than people half his age. It was the things he was excited about that kept him going. You should try that."

He looked at her. *What AM I excited about?* he wondered. He had no idea. "Easter Island, Chorazin, the ruins of Babylon? Those

22

places all have very sinister reputations. It sounds like the topic that most *excited* Jerry is the occult."

She almost giggled. "You got that right. But he wasn't, like, a devil-worshiper or anything like that; I mean, he didn't dress up in a black cloak and sacrifice goats and shit. But, yeah, Jerry believed in the supernatural, all right."

Tilling nodded with a faintly sarcastic smile. "And that is where the distinction lies, I'm afraid, between myself and your friend Jerry. I most certainly do *not* believe in any conceivable avenue of the supernatural."

"That's because you've probably lived your whole life with your head in the sand," she suggested, fiddling with a fingernail.

"I beg your pardon? You don't know anything about me."

"Don't have to. It's obvious. You're an egghead, a dude all wrapped up in his books. That's the only life you know...er, no offense."

Tilling didn't know if he *should* be offended, or not. *I AM an egghead, and for the entirely of my adulthood I HAVE been all wrapped up in books...* "Well...," he began.

"Just tell me this," came her next remark. Now she was leaning forward where she sat, crossing her wrists between her legs. The act pressed her breasts together in a manner that left Tilling no choice but to cast an overt look at them. *Damn*, he thought, hoping he wasn't blushing. Tilling, not at all a sexual being, began to feel stirred. Finally she continued with her next remark: "What's the most exciting thing you've ever done in your life?"

The question turned Tilling, like Lot's wife Edith, into a pillar of salt. The wheels of his consciousness spun madly for an answer but it took him many moments to come up with one. "In 1965, I got to see Mickey Mantle."

Tevi's face twisted up. *"Who?"*

"Mickey— A very famous baseball player. My father took me to Yankee Stadium."

Tevi's shoulders fell and her mouth hung open. "Are you fucking *shitting* me? That's all you got? Seeing some dickbrain baseball player ages ago?"

"It wasn't *ages*, for God's sake," Tilling sniped back.

She seemed on the verge of laughter. "Damn, man, that sucks. I feel sorry for you. Your life's almost over and you haven't even really lived it."

"Thanks a lot," Tilling bristled.

"I mean, no offense."

"Oh, none taken, I assure you!" he almost yelled. "Now you tell *me*, Little Miss Priss. What's the most exciting thing *you've* ever done? Can you tell me that?"

"Oh, that's easy," she replied. "I don't even have to think about it. It was, I think, two Aprils ago. I went down to the chancel with Jerry, and at exactly midnight I smoked some of that stuff he whipped up..."

She paused—Tilling felt sure—for effect. His patience began to percolate; she was toying with him again. "You're a devious and cruel storyteller, Tevi—keeping the old jackass in suspense, is that it? What happened when you smoked Jerry's *stuff* down in the *chancel?*"

"Well, I didn't go on a vision quest. It was nothing like that." Now she seemed to falter at some memory. "I didn't meet an Animal Guide or a Spirit Walker, and it wasn't anything like an out of body experience where your consciousness floats up to the ceiling and you look down and see your physical body and, no, I wasn't transported to the Happy Hunting Ground. That's not where I went."

A scowl now seemed to bake into Tilling's face. "Then where *did* you go?"

"I went straight to Hell," she said.

Tevi had to leave shortly thereafter, and Tilling still couldn't quite read the nature of her intent. Was she stringing him along because she hoped to coax more money out of him? It didn't seem likely because the amount she'd asked for—thirty dollars—wasn't very much these days. When she turned to the front door, Tilling felt dazed by the voluptuous image of her sleek tanned legs and cringingly attractive butt, that and the compelling information she'd related. "I need to hear the rest of the story!" he implored.

"I can't now, my cab's almost here," she said. "I gotta get a move on before rush hour or the driver'll shit a brick. I live all the way over in Kenneth City."

Tilling, irritated, gave her the money he'd promised. "A cab to Kenneth City *has* to cost more than thirty dollars!"

"Calm down, jeez." Tevi tucked the cash into the front pocket of her jeans, her hip cocked forward. "It doesn't cost me anything," she said and winked. "I suck the driver's dick. I *know* I must give good head because—fuck—once he drove me all the way to Orlando and all he wanted was a blow job. That's over a hundred-dollar fare!"

All these irrelevant details on the side were just distracting Tilling; between that, and what she'd just told him, and simply the look of her body, he couldn't think straight. Next she scribbled on a piece of paper and gave it to him. "Here's my number in case you want to see me again—"

"I very much *do* want to see you again," he blurted. "I need to hear the rest of your—"

"Okay, great." She opened the front door and peeked out for a sign of her ride. "I'll come back tomorrow around three. For another thirty dollars, right?"

"Yes, fine—"

"And you might as well throw in another twenty so I can weed whack the high spots in your shitty yard. Otherwise, the neighbors'll complain, and some of 'em are real assholes, trust me—"

"Okay, yes—"

She smiled and her eyes beamed. "Great! See ya tomorrow!" and then she gave him a peck on the cheek and slipped out the front door just as a cab pulled up.

That is one high energy woman, Tilling thought. Once she'd gone, he felt exhausted and invigorated at the same time. Of course he didn't believe her claim to have envisioned Hell while on a drug trip with Jerry, but he could believe that *she* believed it. *She hooked up with this Jerry character, some kook interested in occultism, and she smoked psychedelic drugs with him after he'd already told her the activity would enable her to see the underworld. Then, based on her*

25

preconceived notions of Hell, her brain simply provided an impressive hallucination. It was not a profound conclusion but he had to admit, it was pretty interesting.

And since his retirement, absolutely *nothing* interesting was taking place in his life. He lengthened the thought rather dismally: *Maybe nothing interesting has EVER taken place in my life...*

In the light of that cheerless consideration, it struck him as odd that he should find himself in such elevated spirits. With the last of his blood relations long dead, and no wife, no ex-wife, and no children, he had essentially *no one* of significance in his life now. What was retirement, really, to a solitary man, but just a waiting period for death? He should be down in the proverbial dumps but...

I'm not! he thought in a spark of vivacity.

Of course, it was the girl, it was Tevi. *So what if she's working me? So what if she looks at me like an easy mark?* All of a sudden, just because she'd knocked on his door, Tilling's life was taking on some composure of interest. *I just found out the house I bought used to be owned by an occultist, and the magic carpet of that information is this young, bubbly, and really great-looking girl who's coming back tomorrow!*

Tilling immediately realized that he was sexually aroused—a rare event in his decidedly *un*sexualized life. Fog filled his mind as he set up his laptop, then squinted at the paper with the password for the wifi he'd just had installed yesterday. *Tevi said she did porn back in her drug days,* he couldn't help but recall. *'Look it up on Clips for Sale, and my stuff should pop right up.'* Tilling had no idea what Clips for Sale was but a simple Google took him right to it: a colossal and labyrinthine website full of untold pornographic video clips. In the MODEL SEARCH box, his fingers typed in TEVI, hit Enter, and then there it all bloomed before his eyes. Pornography was something a man like Tilling had been scarcely aware of, but what he saw now seemed beyond his ability to cogitate. A listing of dozens of clips surfaced, each with little thumbnails of a girl who was undoubtedly Tevi, engaged in all manner of sexual conduct. He'd never heard of *bukkake* but here was a clip with the caption: "Smoking hot fuck-tart

Tevi gets slopped up hard by 30 horny studs!" and a pic of buck-naked Tevi lying spread-legged on a table, smiling in disbelief as a half-circle of seedy-looking men masturbated on her. It looked like dozens of sea gulls had excreted on her. "Thar She Blows!" another clip was entitled, with multiple thumbnails showing Tevi on her knees, performing fellatio on one swollen erection after the next. A final jpeg showed Tevi wearing a nearly full *mask* of viscous, white semen, so thick that her eyes, inenose, and mouth couldn't be seen. Yet another clip—called "The Doctor is IN!"—showed naked Tevi sprawled on an exam table with her ankles in stirrups. "Big Doc Spike Wilson delivers the goods to everybody's favorite cum-dump Tevi!" This one showed a preview-type tiff file of a man in a labcoat standing between Tevi's opened legs and rocking a preposterously large erection in and out of the girl's rather petite genitals.

This...isn't what I expected, came Tilling's crestfallen conclusion. There was nothing erotic about such depictions, and as he scrolled farther down the list, the revelations proved even less promising. Tevi being sodomized somehow by two men at a time, Tevi being "gang-banged," Tevi swallowing a juice glass full of sperm, Tevi being urinated on by men and women alike.

That's enough of that, Tilling concluded and turned it off. He didn't want to see Tevi subjecting herself to such harrowing abasement. It was out and out depressing but the worst part was, getting to see Tevi fully naked left Tilling with no choice. He masturbated right there on the couch, feeling utterly imbecilic. It was the first time he'd done so in longer than he could remember.

God, I hope she comes back tomorrow, he caught himself thinking. But he had to wonder what his motives were. She'd been a porn model and had asserted just as nonchalantly that she was not averse to acts of prostitution. But Tilling knew that this notion was *not* the reason he was so suddenly taken by her. *No way,* he thought. *I'd feel ridiculous. I'd be too self-conscious. I probably wouldn't even be able to get it up, I'd be so nervous...*

No, there'd be none of that. He supposed what was happening was nothing more complicated than a boring old man having a crush on a vibrant, attractive girl much younger than himself. And when he looked at it that way, he felt satisfied to think, *Big deal? So what? It's harmless so don't worry about it.*

Next he Googled Jerry Orne and then Jeronymous Orne. Nothing intelligible came back for his efforts, and he was too impatient to pursue a more intricate search. He knew there was a way to search real estate transaction records and property taxes but— *To hell with it. I don't know how to do that...*

He skipped his frequent microwave dinner and, after nightfall, when he would ordinarily be tuning in to whatever inane movie was available from whatever ad-laden streaming service, he found himself limping right back down the steps to the basement. This time he'd unboxed one of those caged light bulbs on an extension cord, which he dragged into the hidden room and hung up. The added illumination lessened the cubby's previously foreboding cast. The moldy smell remained, along with that smoky scent. Here he made a closer examination of the jars and boxes on the plastic shelves. He opened the first cigar box, withdrew the stone-bowled pipe, and sniffed the charred residue inside. *Not bad*, he thought. There was a redolence of something like cedar mixed with basil. The other boxes housed more pipes and some lighters. *Now, what exactly might this be?* he wondered of the biggest jar on the shelf. It was full of dried leaves and tiny withered flowers, and another jar was full of granules or powder of some sort. He opened both jars and sniffed: the first smelled like dried leaves in a forest, and the second had an odd bacon-like scent. But the next jar gave him reason to pause before opening it. *Doesn't look exactly pleasant*, he thought. It resembled lumpy tar with a purplish or maroonish cast. It took a few tries but when he finally opened it, he detected a charry herbal scent like that of the stone pipe. *So this must be Jerry's secret concoction derived from photocopies of languages I'm wholly ignorant of...* Or perhaps the photocopies were of manuscripts that were fabricated. *There's a sucker born every minute and maybe Jerry was one of them, and he bought the pages from some charlatan posing as an antiquary.* It didn't matter. People would believe anything they wanted to...

Tilling tried to watch TV later but fell asleep in short order. Snatches of dreams kept waking him up, images of Tevi no doubt borrowed from the porn site, but *these* images went much farther than the real jpegs and tiffs, and they were mixed with a bit of morbid fancy. Tilling's dreaming mind stared at a stripped naked Tevi being sexually mauled in every way imaginable: forced fellatio, rampant sodomy, fisting, piss parties, and the like, and all the while Tevi herself was grinning in glee.

But it was not men doing these things to her, it was demons.

Tilling was up early. He'd passed a lousy night due to the sickening salvo of nightmares but he was unable to sleep in. He was too excited: Tevi was coming back today, and this thought jolted him with energy. Not knowing what she might want, he had coffee and donuts delivered, then he proceeded to pace back and forth in the living room, frequently peeping out the front window for signs of her cab. As three o'clock drew near, he was standing in the open doorway, tapping his foot. *Jesus, I'm like a little kid at Christmas waiting for Santa...*

When she finally arrived, she was thrilled by the coffee and donuts that he'd set out on the table. "You rock," she exclaimed with her mouth full. "I didn't have anything in the fridge for breakfast."

Tilling nodded obliquely, sipping his coffee and failing at a concerted effort not to stare at her body. *For pity's sake, she's built...* She wore cutoffs and clunky work boots, and she had an orange t-shirt on over—to Tilling's disappointment—her impressive bosom satcheled up in a bra. He was about to invite her to sit down on the couch, to continue yesterday's conversation, when she said rather abruptly, "Let me get the dull stuff out of the way first," and she scurried down to the basement before Tilling could even ask what she was doing. She bounded right back up a minute later, holding the battery powered weed-whacker. "This won't take long," she said. Tilling was about to tell her not to bother, but, in a wink's time, she'd pulled off the orange t-shirt to reveal breasts sitting heavily in not a

29

bra but an orange bikini top. Before Tilling could get a word in, she was out the door and going at it with the weed-whacker.

Suddenly his mind was awash in questions. *What else was her experience with Jerry? The one time she'd smoked the drugs or whatever they were...what did she really see? And what about Jerry himself? 'Jerry smoked it dozens of times,' she said, or hundreds. What had he told her of his own experiences?*

He couldn't wait to talk to her. It was maddening that he had to wait for her to do something as mundane as cutting the grass. But he had to wait still more when she finally finished and came back in, her tan skin shining in sweat. "I'm gonna take a shower, okay?" and before he could reply she strode off for the bathroom. The hiss of the shower was almost hypnotizing; he was actually dozing off on the couch when her voice roused him, "Sorry, but where are the towels? The closet's empty." His eyes shot open when he saw her leaning unabashed out into the hallway, one half of her naked body clearly visible. He tried to act unaffected when he got up and rooted through the boxes where he thought more towels were. When he walked toward her to give her one, she stepped fully into view. Tilling could've keeled over. *My God, what a knockout. That is one beautiful woman.* Straight wet black hair lay behind her shoulders, exposing the large sagless breasts centered with caramel-colored nipples the size of poker chips. What heightened the erotic image were the rough tan-lines from her shorts and bikini top. That and the sharp dark eyes and jet-black tuft of pubic hair seemed to condense the entirety of her physique into a short, voluptuous statue.

She rolled her eyes as she nonchalantly dried herself. "What? You've never seen a naked woman before?"

"Well, not many, and none as uniquely attractive as you."

"Come on. All those hot college girls you taught? I'll bet they were crawling all over you for that A-plus."

"Believe me, I'm disconsolate to inform you that no such thing even came close to ever happening to me," Tilling admitted, but he had to wonder, if any such opportunities had presented themselves, what would he have done?

Probably nothing. Just a boring, bald stick in the mud. Shit...

Back in her tight shorts and top, she flopped down on the couch. "So...I forgot. You wanted to know about Jerry's jaunts, right?"

"His jaunts?"

"That's what he called it. Whenever he'd smoke his stuff downstairs and do the ritual, he called it going on a *jaunt.*"

"A drug trip," Tilling supposed.

"If that's the way you need to think of it then, fine. But it was more than, like, dropping acid." She crossed her ankles and put her long tan legs up on the coffee table. "You ever done acid, mescaline, mushrooms, stuff like that?"

The idea was laughable. "*Me?* For pity's sake, no."

Tevi smiled. "Yeah, I guess that was a dumb question. A party machine you ain't. But Jerry's jaunts didn't take place in your head the way LSD and the other stuff does. It takes you somewhere *beyond* your head. You won't believe that but it's true."

"You mean Hell. You smoke the drugs and you see Hell," Tilling said more than asked.

Now she was inspecting her nails. "You don't just see it, you *go there.* But like I said, you'll never believe it, not a guy like you. The only way you'd ever believe it is if you did it."

Tilling chuckled. "I'd say the chances of that happening present a very *low* order of possibility."

She shrugged. "That's too bad. I think you'd appreciate the experience."

It was more unconscious than anything when Tilling continued to be the naysayer. "Yes, of course, but such an *experience* is actually only mental imagery concocted by chemicals in the brain."

She grinned at him. "Yeah, I guess you've been living in the box so long, it's too late to get out—"

Tilling frowned; it sounded like an insult but then it didn't seem that she'd intended that.

"People live a certain kind of life, they get so set in their own ways that they can't imagine that there's any other kind of reality out there. My people are the same way. We became so set on the ideas we'd believed for thousands of years that we couldn't imagine anything else. Then the white missionaries came along and tried to ram Christianity down our throats. How'd that work out? We didn't buy that any more than you can buy this. Everybody's got their own ideas based on what was handed down by their own cultures. Shit, most Native American tribes didn't even believe that Hell existed. There was no word for it, there was no concept of it. Fuck, I didn't believe in Heaven *or* Hell. I thought it was just shit that stupid people made up because they needed to believe there was something more than just this shitty life on this shitty planet. So they invented God, and they invented a place where you go after you die, where you live forever, but only if you're good. If you're bad—well, they had to invent something for that too. The place for *bad* people to go when you die. Obey the rules or else. Conform or else. They had to invent that place too."

"Spoken like a true atheist!" Tilling exclaimed.

She frowned. "No, no, man—you're not hearing me. I mean that's what I *used* to believe, that it was all a crock of shit that people made up. But now I know it's not. Now I know it's real. Hate to say it, but the missionaries were right."

"Hell, you mean," Tilling clarified. "Now you know that *Hell* is real—"

"Yeah, because I've fuckin' seen it." Suddenly her gaze bored into his. "Shit, I'd love to see your reaction if you went on a jaunt."

"You really think I'd believe it was more than hallucination?"

"You'd have to." Now she raised her toned arms over her head and stretched. "Then you'd be *really* fucked up. You're the kind of guy who couldn't face the idea what everything you've ever believed is wrong. It would make your entire life meaningless. Everything you've ever learned, everything you've ever taught, all that knowledge— None of it's worth a pinch of shit."

Tilling was close to throwing some back at her but... *What if she's right?* He tried to focus his thoughts to effectively argue with her but he couldn't, he was too distracted by the perspective of her body all stretched out like that. "Well, young lady, it sounds like you're challenging me, like you're *daring* me to do one of these, these *jaunts*."

She jerked her gaze to him as if very concerned. "Oh, no, man. Don't ever do anything just because someone else tells you to. You gotta make up your own mind."

Her pose relaxed; her perfect breasts settled in the orange top over her flat stomach. Tilling almost cringed now, at the potency of that image of her. *My God...*

"But," she began again, "aren't you even a little curious?"

"Yes," came his immediate answer, "but not quite curious enough to inhale toxic, unknown chemicals into my body."

She nodded, half smiling and, next, she voiced his exact thought of a moment ago: "But what if I'm right, huh? Isn't there some itsy bitsy little part of your super-smart college-professor brain that *has* to wonder?"

In the next fraction of a moment, Tilling's consciousness felt as though it were being siphoned away into some primal void of self-reflection. What was he exactly? A decent person, a moral man who'd been raised well and had grown up in positive environments; he was preeminently educated and impeccably civilized. Now, however, these qualities corroded to nothingness, leaving only a raw, lustful primitive *thing* that wanted to rage against this petite woman on his couch who was taunting him sexually and reveling in bringing him down. He wanted to crack her hard across the face, then yank her shorts off against her will and push his face between her legs and lick her there voraciously. He wanted to grab her throat and squeeze and yell and tear off her top, ply her awesome breasts, and jerk off on her stomach. Then he wanted to—

The mad spill of shrieking thoughts evaporated at once. *Where the hell did all that come from?* he thought desperately, blinking till his eyes hurt. He stared at her, and answered her question on in a single gruff "Yes."

"You wouldn't really be human if you didn't," she said.

Fuck it, he thought, and got up and strode to the kitchen. He fetched a cup and poured himself some wine. "You want some?"

Tevi laughed. "It's a little early for me. I thought you didn't drink."

"I do today."

She peered at him, her head tilted. "Am I shaking you up, knocking you off track?"

"No," he said. The wine tasted exquisite. "I'm simply celebrating."

She sat up and swiveled toward him, enthused. "Celebrating what?"

"You being here."

"Really?"

"Yes. You're fascinating." He closed his eyes, looking upward, trying to think of the right words. "You induce me to make a deeper disquisitional survey of myself."

"The *fuck?*"

"Everything you've said since we met makes me see the truth about myself."

Her eyes lit up. "Well, that's good, isn't it?"

"The truth is always good—at least that's what the philosophers tell us. And I very much suspect you had the same effect on Jerry."

Now she was sitting on crossed legs, her satcheled breasts hanging at a perfect angle. "I don't know if I had any real *effect* on Jerry, I mean, other than making him come. But he liked me because he liked talking to me and I did stuff for him. He trusted me to sit with him."

"Ah, that again," Tilling said, the subject rekindled. "What exactly do you mean by *sitting* with him?"

"You know. Whenever he did a jaunt, he had me sit with him, in case something went wrong. He wanted me there in case he had a heart attack or something. Before I flushed my life down the toilet grinding pills, I was taking EMT classes at the community college. I know how to do CPR and shit."

Tilling looked at her more intently. "Did that ever happen?"

"Couple times," she said. "I told you, the guy was *old*. Once or twice the shit he saw on the other side—"

The other side, Tilling repeated the words.

"—was too much for him and his heart stopped. But I got it back up and running again." Her brows shot up and she giggled. "See? At least there's one thing I can do right: bring old guys back to life!"

Tilling recognized the allegorical significance of her statement. Now his cognition seemed to be ticking. "So that's what sitting is... An ethereal babysitter. But earlier, didn't you say something about a *ritual*? Is sitting part of that?"

"The whole thing is part of a ritual, yeah. But me sitting with Jerry wasn't part of it. That was just a safety measure.."

"Then what exactly does the ritual involve? Tell me, step by step. Please."

"Wow, you really *are* interested in this stuff, aren't you?"

Tilling shrugged. "Well, yes. You're the one who knocked on my door, remember? Offering unique knowledge?"

"Yep." She sprang up from the couch. "Come on, I'll show you how he did it," and then she grabbed Tilling's hand and coaxed him to the steps down to the basement.

She addressed the jars on the white plastic shelf, touching each one as she named it: "Lophop, jimson, vervain, Lady's Mantle," she said, then she touched another smaller jar full of brown star-shaped flowers. "Star anise. It kind of guns up the connection between the Living World and the other side—you know, like squirting lighter fluid on a fire. And these," she said of another jar, "I'm sure you've seen 'em before—dried cloves. You burn them in a censer bowl. It keeps anything from over there from fucking with you over here."

Tilling stared at the jars without really seeing them. "Over there, meaning Hell," he said.

Tevi nodded.

"Has that happened? Something from over there coming here?"

"Nope. Because we always burned cloves before the ritual." She seemed to relay the information as if it were utterly commonplace. Tilling was starting to surface from his mental fog. *How much of this does she really believe?* he wondered. *All of it? Burning cloves keeps devils at bay?*

"It's kind of like bug spray," she continued. "They don't like it so they don't try anything. Okay, and...there's *this*." Now her fingertip landed on the jar that seemed full of purplish-red paste that he'd opened earlier. "Looks gross but it doesn't smell bad," she informed. "This is the main stuff—"

"The admixture whose ingredients Jerry derived from the photocopied manuscripts upstairs—I should say the *unreadable* manuscripts."

"*Jerry* could read 'em. That's all that mattered."

Tilling's gaze thinned. "Did Jerry, by chance, happen to leave any notes behind, or a diary maybe?"

"No, I told you. He wouldn't leave anything written down—it was too dangerous, he said. He didn't want the secrets in those papers upstairs to wind up in the hands of the wrong people, so he never wrote *anything* down. He memorized everything he needed, along with the invocation."

"Invocation," Tilling repeated. "An orison, you mean?"

"A what?"

"A prayer or benediction that's said aloud—"

She nodded. "Yeah. According to Jerry it has to be said out loud or it won't work."

"So..." It took several moments for Tilling to actually present her with his next question. "Did *you* memorize the invocation?"

This time her pretty smile seemed a little dark, or maybe that was only because of the wedges of darkness in the basement. "No, I didn't memorize it. But you're starting to sound like you might actually want to do a jaunt yourself."

I'd be INSANE to do a 'jaunt,' his thoughts snapped back. *Inhaling toxic, hallucinatory substances? I would NEVER do anything so stupid!* But he did not directly respond to her comment. "Just tell me this, Tevi. Earlier you said you did it once, right? But that you'd never do it again?"

"Yeah."

"Why not? It sounds like an extraordinary experience—"

A smirk contorted her otherwise pretty face. "It was extraordinary, all right. Shit. Once was good enough for me. Let's just say...I saw something there, something I didn't need to see. It fucked me up."

"So, what? What did you see that was so disturbing?"

Her face went blank. She looked right at him and shook her head.

"Okay, then. So even if you wanted to do another jaunt, or if I wanted to—it couldn't be done, could it?"

"It could easily be done—"

Now Tilling guessed he was trying to trip her up in her fabrications. "How? The manuscripts are undecipherable and untranslated, and you didn't memorize the invocation that makes the ritual work."

"Still think I'm full of shit, huh?" she said, regaining that smile. "I didn't need to memorize the invocation. One time when Jerry was saying it, I recorded it behind his back." She held up her cellphone.

"I must say, you're quite industrious!" Tilling told her.

Tevi shrugged. "I'm not even sure why I made the recording, 'cos I already knew I'd never do another jaunt again."

"In the event you might change your mind?"

"I don't know. Fuck. Maybe. Yeah, I guess."

Tilling's head filled with a drone. What was wrong with him? What was he thinking? His attention had divided and sub-divided so many times by now that he didn't know which iota to focus on. But there in the middle of it all stood Tevi: tan, voluptuous, and raunchily beautiful with her breasts pushing out against the orange top, revealing shadows of large nipples, the tight cut-off shorts loudly displaying the cleft of her sex. Tilling couldn't take his eyes off her, nor could he stop hearing in his mind some of her previous remarks.

—you've been living in the box so long, it's too late to get out—

—you've probably lived your whole life with your head in the sand—

—to learn things he was interested in. His life's adventure—

"Are you all right?" she asked.

His lips parted. He felt very far away. "I..."

Tevi's brow rose; now her smile seemed coy. "Your cock is hard. I can see it through your damn pants, man..."

Now the drone rose to a high-frequency note, only to drop back down again to an almost sub-octave hum. He tried to say something but couldn't; he could only continue to gaze at her.

"If you want it that bad, you can have it," she said. She took off her top. "I won't even charge you."

The big brown nipples stared back at him, like eyes. "No, damn it, I'm sorry. But I think I..."

"You think what?"

"I think..."

She was grinning. "Yeah?"

The drone stopped as abruptly as a car crash. "I think I want to do what you and Jerry did," Tilling said in a voice the sounded famished. "I think I want to go on a jaunt."

Tevi had taken two of the cigar boxes off the plastic shelf, and then led Tilling back upstairs. All of a sudden she'd become very quiet, and seemed almost solemn. Tilling himself felt rather jittery; he knew, as he sat down on the couch staring ahead, that he was going to do this, against every fiber of his better judgment. It was stupid, crazy, and very dangerous but—

I'm going to do it anyway. Fuck it.

When she came back from the kitchen, she'd put her orange bikini top back on. In one hand she held her paper cup full of more wine, and in the other hand she held a knife—just an ordinary kitchen steak knife with a brown plastic handle. His first impulse was to ask her why she had a knife...but he didn't. *I'll find out in due time,* he reasoned. Instead, he asked, "We're going to do it downstairs, right? In Jerry's 'chancel?' Why did you bring me back up here?"

"To talk," she said, sitting down next to him. Eventually she put the knife down. Gone were her sultry smiles, her wide gazes, and her lackadaisical demeanor. "There are things you need to know if you decide to go through with this."

"I've already decided—"

"Are you *sure?*" she demanded. "This shit's no joke. Maybe you think it is but it's not."

"I don't think it's a joke, Tevi," he said in a dry monotone. "And I'm sure. I'm absolutely certain that I want to do it."

She shook her head and looked at him. She seemed disgruntled. "Fuck. Now that I've thought about it more, I honestly have to advise you *not* to do it."

Tilling winced. "That's ridiculous! You told me it was the best experience of your life!"

"Yeah, and what did I tell you after that? That I'd never do it again. It was horrifying. I don't think you could handle it. If you kicked off, it would be *my* fuckin' fault."

He actually chuckled now. "For pity's sake, I'm not going to *kick off*—"

She slouched back and put her feet back up on the coffee table, her arms crossed under her breasts. "What the fuck was I thinking? I never should've dredged this up—"

"Ah, but you *did*, so let's get on with it," he said almost testily.

"There's shit that you need to understand." She glowered straight ahead; she appeared very displeased with herself. "Hell itself, for one thing."

"What do you mean?"

"What exactly do you think Hell is?" she asked. "You think it's some big smoking fire-pit full of demons with horns and pitchforks?"

That's a good question, he admitted to himself. An hour ago he was certain that there was no afterlife, no Heaven, no Hell. Now, however? Tevi's implications about her exploits with Jerry Orne had scored rents into these certainties. But if he was going to consider that he might be wrong...

How *did* he conceive of Hell? What might it really be like?

"I...don't know how to answer that," he said. "A void of darkness, maybe? An immense perimeter of—I don't know... Fire? Heat?"

"No, man. You're way off base. Let me put it this way. What's the biggest city in the world? New York? Chicago?"

"No," Tilling answered. Here was something he knew. "Either Tokyo or Delhi, I think."

"Okay, whatever. What was Tokyo like ten thousand years ago?"

Tilling gave it some thought. "Just woodland, probably. Populated by small groups of hunter-gatherers and cave-dwellers."

"Great. And in the time between then and now, that same area has evolved into one of the biggest cities on earth, right?"

"Exactly."

"And the same with every other city, right? Every other city on earth?"

"Well, yes. Every city, every place with any kind of a population. Ten thousand years ago, there *were* no cites."

"But since then, human civilization has grown, it's evolved in a huge way, right?"

"Yes, it has," Tilling agreed. "But what do such observations have to do with *Hell?*"

"Everything," she said, looking at him. "Just as human civilization has evolved over the last ten thousand years, so has Hell. And why wouldn't it? It makes sense, doesn't it?"

Tilling shrugged. "I suppose it does."

"Of course it does. Everything grows, everything becomes more advanced, everything becomes bigger and better over time. Hell's no different. Ten thousand years ago, Hell was a wasteland full of caves and crevices and holes with smoke pouring out of them. But what do you think it is *now?*"

He stared off into the blank wall. *Be deductive*, he told himself. *What had she first been asking about? Cities?*

"A...city?" he ventured.

She clapped her hands once very loud. "Yes! A city, a *giant* city that's been growing and evolving since way back when, just like civilization's been growing and evolving here. Hell is a city, all right, and it's called the Mephistopolis—"

The strange word seemed to drift around inside Tilling's head. *Mephistopolis—*

"—and it's so big that if you took every city on earth and put them together, the Mephistopolis is bigger than 'em all, ten—no, a *hundred* times bigger."

Tilling thought about that, tried to picture it, but couldn't.

She opened one of the cigar boxes and held up the pipe with the stone bowl. "That's what's waiting for you at the end of this pipe, a city bigger than anything you can imagine, and more horrible. There are things in the Mephistopolis that—" She stopped. "Well, if you're really gonna do it, you'll see for yourself."

"Have no doubt," Tilling affirmed. "I'm really going to do it. So let's stop all this fooling around. I want to do it *now.*"

She craned her neck to look out the front window. It was just now getting dark. "We have to wait till midnight—"

"Midnight?" he snapped. "Why?"

"The Witching Hour and all that—"

Tilling almost laughed. "Oh, for pity's sake. That's so hokey! Next you'll be telling me we have to burn black candles—"

"The candles can be any color. And it's gotta be midnight, because Jerry said so. That's the way it is so you gotta go with it. Don't doubt it, don't shit on it, *just go with it.* You think you know fuckin' better—well, guess what. You *don't.* People have been doing shit like this for thousands of years—at *midnight.* What? You're right, and they're all wrong?" She was obviously getting mad. "Yeah, I'll bet you *do* think that. Big Mr. Professor, Mr. Know It All. But what's all that got you now, huh? Jack shit. If you want to do this, you gotta do it right. If you doubt it, it won't work. If you think it's hokey, fine, don't do it. I'm serious. *Don't* do it."

She's right. I AM a know it all. I'm a conceited old snoot. "Tevi, your message has been received loud and clear."

"Good," she said abruptly. "Stop being a dick." Her breasts depended flawless in the bikini top when she reached over and picked up the second cigar box. "First thing we gotta do is make your Ambix—"

"Ambix?" Tilling said, stretching the word. *What an odd thing to say...* "You mean the Greek word?"

"How the fuck do I know if it's fuckin' *Greek?*" she said. She opened the cigar box in her lap. This box was formerly for White Owls.

"You speak with the eloquence of queens." Tilling smiled. "Ambix is Greek for cup or vessel. Something that carries or holds something else."

"Well, I guess that makes sense then." Inside the White Owl box were several much smaller boxes—about one inch square—made of unfinished pine. Atop one the letter T had been written in magic marker; atop another, the letter J.

"T for Tevi?" Tilling guessed. "J for Jerry?"

"That's right," she said. She picked up the magic marker, uncapped it, then picked up an unmarked box. "What's your first name?"

"Herman," Tilling said.

Tevi smiled to herself. "Yep. That's an egghead name, all right."

"Just call me Tilling."

She drew an H on the unmarked box. "Now we have to make your Ambix." She opened J and removed a peculiar pendant: marble-sized, round but irregular, oddly glittery. As it swung from her fingertips on a silver chain, the stone seemed to shift from reddish-purple to greenish-yellow.

"This is the Ambix we made for Jerry. It's a special kind of gem stone, but I can't remember the name. Jerry said witches and warlocks have been using them for ages."

Tilling made an effort not to frown at the witches and warlocks reference. "It's a beautiful stone. It might be alexandrite—"

"That's it," Tevi acknowledged.

"—and I believe it's rather rare and can be quite expensive."

"I'll say." She opened a fourth box, which contained more such stones. "Jerry said they cost fifteen grand each."

She let him hold the chain. The incandescent lamps in the living room caused a tumult of color-changes in the stone; it was uncanny. "I'm no expert, but I think these are higher quality alexandrites. I've seen them in museums." He glanced over at her. "I suspect you could sell these to a gemologist for a considerable sum."

Tevi glared at him. "They're not *mine*, man. Damn. I'm not a fuckin' thief—"

"I'm sure you're not," Tilling agreed, peering more closely at the stone. "I was merely pointing out the possibility. It's absolutely gorgeous."

"Yeah. Jerry said they're from the Oral Mountains. Who the fuck would name mountains *oral?*"

Tilling forestalled laughter. "I think Jerry meant the *Ural* Mountains, in Russia."

"Whatever, oral, Ural, who gives a fuck?"

He squinted more closely, now noticing some sort of blemish or scratches on the sides of the stone. "It looks like—"

"Jerry used an engraver to drill some pits in it."

"Why?"

"To hold the blood."

Tilling shot her a sharp glance. "Blood?"

"Yeah. Your blood's gotta stay on the stone. If it goes in the pits, it won't wipe off."

"So I've got to *cut* myself?"

"That's right," she replied as if the prospect were nothing. "Then smear your blood on the stone."

She took the pendant—the *Ambix*—from Tilling, put it back in its box, then removed a similar pendant from the H-marked box, handed it to Tilling, and then handed him the knife. "Go on."

Tilling frowned. He put the point of the knife to his fingertip, then pushed and twisted, but couldn't quite summon the requisite bravado to puncture his skin. "Damn it, I-I don't think I can do it."

Tevi slid over right next to him, her thigh against his. "What a cream-cake," she chuckled. She took the knife, grabbed his hand and—

"Oww!"

—pierced his fingertip. A bead of bright blood welled up.

"Rub it all around the stone, especially over the pits Jerry drilled, then set it aside so it can dry."

Tilling followed her instructions, embarrassed that he couldn't even prick his own finger.

She'd run off to the kitchen, returned with a paper towel, then sat back down next to him and daubed paltry wound.

"What now?" Tilling asked.

"Now we watch TV till midnight." Her eyes lit up. "Do you have Netflix?"

Back down to the basement they went at about 11:30 pm. Tevi, first, lit the six candles on the floor, then reset and wound the small mantle clock on the plastic shelf. Next she pulled up the straw mats on the floor to reveal—

"What?" Tilling said. "No pentagrams?"

Painted on the floor, rather expertly, was an odd configuration that had quite an "occult" look to it, but nothing he'd ever seen before. It was a double circle inside of which were two uneven right-angled lines.

"It's called the Senary Sigil," Tevi said, and then she bent over and placed a candle at the ends of each line and at the joints of the angles.

Six candles on the six points of the sigil—the devil's number, he thought, refraining his typical sarcastic smile. But he didn't voice his opinion this time. *I already pissed her off once. I better not do it again...*

"Okay, we're almost ready." When she went to place the pendant around Tilling's neck, her fantastic breasts rose, then fell. Tilling couldn't help but notice, and the area of his groin couldn't help but respond. *Damn it, not another boner...* But things, in this respect, were about to get worse—

She took off her orange bikini top again, and then—

Why's she doing that?

—stepped out of her cutoff shorts, pantiless beneath.

Tilling could not will himself to look away from her impeccable physique.

"It's best for us to be naked," she said. "Jerry used to say that nudity is the best way to solicit the Devil. Satan likes to see his subjects naked."

Tilling's eyes bugged. "No, no, there's no way I'm taking my clothes off. One thing I can guarantee you, the Devil doesn't want to see *me* naked! You? *Of course.* But not *me.* It would piss him off..."

Tevi's bare shoulders rose and fell. "Well, okay. We'll work with what we've got." In the wavering candlelight she put her hands on his shoulders, guided him around, and told him to sit down at the head of the circle. "It's best to sit in a lotus position," she said, then walked to the plastic shelves.

Tilling grimaced, manipulating himself to sit accordingly. "I'm too old to sit in a lotus position!"

"Just do it and quit whining..."

Eventually, Tilling managed to do as instructed, quite uncomfortably, and the erection that raged in his pants didn't help. When he looked behind him in the shifting shadows, he saw Tevi standing at the shelves; one of the jars was open, and she was tamping some of that purple-reddish paste into the pipe with the stone bowl. A moment later she was sitting opposite him. In the center of the sigil she placed a small pyramid-shaped object a few inches high; it appeared to be made of copper or bronze, and to its point she applied the flame of a Bic lighter until something began to burn. *The cloves,* Tilling realized. It was an annoying smell. Next Tevi passed him the pipe and the lighter. "Don't light it till I tell you," she said. "And until then, picture the sigil in your mind."

Again, he fought not to frown, He looked down alternately at the ludicrous diagram on the floor and Tevi's perfect naked body across from him. She sat there like someone meditating, looking up with closed eyes, hands aside with thumbs touching index fingers. The flickering candlelight licked frantically over every feature of her body; it somehow made her look possessed of more than three dimensions. Tilling stared at her indefectible breasts, her toned, spread thighs, then her open crotch. He imagined collapsing on top of her, pushing his face between her breasts, sucking her nipples back and forth, then slithering his face down her belly to lick her as intimately as possible. *My God...,* he thought. His erection was beating so frantically in his pants that he feared he'd ejaculate spontaneously. He knew that if she touched him there, just with one finger through his pants, he'd gush sperm and make a big wet spot—

"You're supposed to be thinking about the sigil, not me," she said, but still had her eyes closed. *She's just guessing,* he figured, *but she's right. Shit.* He refocused, closed his eyes tight and framed the image in his mind: the circle with the two angles in it, the shadows from the candles wavering over it, and the tinted darkness around them.

He wondered if there really was a Devil, and if it was true, was the Devil *really* aware of what was going on here? Of course, he couldn't believe it. But as he held the diagram's image more precisely in his mind, he began to feel more and more distant. He received the distinct impression that they were no longer sitting in a cramped cinder-block room in his basement but in a borderless void of infinite black. They were tiny in that void—no, subatomic. Who knew what else might be out there? And if there were *nothing* out there, that was even scarier. The replication of the sigil that he'd made in his mind began to illumine and vibrate. Gradually he became aware of a ticking sound—of course, the mantle clock that Tevi had wound. But what also occurred to him was that it was ticking faster than once per second. The scent of burning cloves was absent now. His eyes opened, it seemed, without a command from his brain. Tevi still sat across from him, the sigil was still on the floor, and the candles were still flickering, only their light seemed white instead of the typical yellow, and it wasn't as bright. He stared intently across at Tevi, waiting for a flinch, a tic, an infinitesimal movement of an eyeball behind the lid—but there was nothing. She may as well have been made of stone...or dead.

Then, behind Tevi, in that illimitable scape of squid-ink blackness, Tilling saw something. His lips parted...

First it was mirage-like, seeming to flux in and out of existence. It was like—

What is that?

It was like staring at an oil painting five hundred years old, from the days when artists would often paint over older paintings in order to reuse a canvas. Sometimes, if the lighting was just right, and the temperature a little warm, and you were looking at the proper angle, a face from the older paint would half-surface into the newer paint...

That's akin to what Tilling saw now, just over Tevi's left shoulder. Hovering behind her at an incalculable distance. It was a face.

It was the most horrific face he could ever have imagined, and also the most beautiful. It was chaotic and lovely, abominable and pristine at the same time. Just as Tilling felt that he would have to stand up and walk to the face—

"Okay. It's about time now—"

The manic ticking instantly reduced to its normal one tick per second pace. The black lines which constructed the sigil's borders appeared wider for some reason Tilling couldn't guess, and the image of Tevi seemed more defined: veins stood out on her arms and neck, her eyes deeper in her skull, her flat stomach flatter, abdominal muscles obvious beneath the skin. It was as if she'd undergone some inexplicable weight loss in mere minutes. Tilling noticed, somehow, more veins beating in her breasts. Her eyes looked slightly larger than real, and famished, cringing for some essential satisfaction, perhaps sexual.

"You look different," he said. "Do I?"

"Shh!" Her eyes stared right into his, like nails driven into his head. She raised her cellphone. "When you start hearing the words, light the pipe, and inhale once very deeply. Do you understand?"

Tilling nodded; when his eyes drooped to her bare crotch, he noticed a wet glimmering.

Her breasts rose and fell once, then she pressed the PLAY button on her cellphone...

First came a hollow static, then a peculiar male voice began to intone words that sounded like: "Zu tod madru gerdab... exinivov unimotid—"

Tilling snapped the lighter and began to light the pipe. As he drew in, the sound of the air being drawn sounded like someone sucking breath in between their teeth. His mouth began to fill with heat that seemed oily...

"—ohan ze ix kasundax damik extrok—"

Tilling kept drawing the smoke into his lungs. He expected a fierce irritation and a propulsive need to cough, but nothing of the sort occurred. A sapor seemed to accommodate the taste of the smoke—licorice and citrus?—

"—badinomn exot exturoz exka ne—"

He couldn't tell when he'd stopped inhaling; he didn't remember any sensation of his lungs filling up. Suddenly he felt weightless, he felt as if he were floating several inches off the floor. His vision wobbled; he was staring directly at Tevi, directly at her mouth, when the incantation finished:

"—gradimox xexari en ixteb tu ma."

Tilling seemed to evaporate in place, shot forward as if made of something gaseous, and disappeared into Tevi's mouth, down her throat, and down farther, deeper, into infinite depths of obsidian blackness. He felt himself corkscrewing as he descended, and he knew he was screaming yet he could hear no sound, and when he brought his hands to his face as if in some useless effort to protect himself, he did not feel any trace of his hands, nor did he see them.

What he *did* see was difficult to think. Was he in a tunnel of utter darkness? *Yes!* he thought, because he could swear there was a tiny egress far up head, like a minuscule dot of red light. He began to soar down this black passage toward it, his velocity trebling every second, until he felt completely out of control. He was screaming again but still unable to hear it. *This must be what it's like when a fighter pilot crashes...* Now that tiny red dot wasn't so tiny; it was shooting right at him like a tracer bullet. Tilling couldn't move, he couldn't affect anything that was happening. All he could do was watch—

He expected to watch his own death but instead—

Holy shiiiiiit!

It felt like he was experiencing a full-body orgasm. His entire being spasmed and pulsed. *My God, my God...* The convulsions of pleasure were denser and more complete than anything he'd ever felt. At the same time he seemed to punch through the red dot into a wide-open space.

Now he lay motionless, but on what he didn't know. Around him stood buildings and shops as might be found on any city street. Was he lying on his back, on asphalt? Again he raised his hands in front of his field of vision but still saw nothing. Very, very gradually, like someone turning a volume knob up very, very slowly, he began to hear things: yelling, people talking, bells, and something like traffic. But then he heard something familiar:

"Okay, here's how it works—" It was Tevi's voice. "You're in the Mephistopolis now—in Hell. Over there you have no physical body—that's back over here with me. The first thing you gotta do is get your sea legs."

My fuckin' SEA LEGS? his thoughts tried to yell back. *I don't even HAVE legs!*

"You gotta get up off the ground before a Bio-Wizard or an Ophitte Sage sees you. Believe me, they'll fuck you up. But the good news is, no one else in Hell can see you. Over there, you're completely discorporate. So get up—"

I can't get up, damn you! I got no legs!

"Just focus real hard and imagine your physical body. You're lying there on your back. Picture that in your brain. And then *picture yourself* getting up."

In the effort to concentrate, Tilling made to close his eyes but couldn't. *Of course not! No eyelids!* Nevertheless, he did his best to imagine his physical body getting up and standing on his own feet. *There! I did it!* and when his vision swerved, he screamed yet again as a horn blared, and what appeared to be a speeding bus drove right into him.

But he felt nothing, no impact. He passed through the bus as it moved over him, and inside he caught glimpses of demonic children kicking and twitching from meat hooks hanging from the ceiling. A lump-faced gray Troll dressed in a police uniform walked casually down the center aisle, *tapping* the end of a billy club in his palm. "Fuckin' Broodren," he said in a Brooklyn accent, "juvenile delinquent pieces'a shit! A man can't have a proper piece of ass without one of you little crotch goblins poppin' out. Yeah, well, we'll fix your wagons. Little fuckers think you can ruin things for *everyone* in Hell." The cop chuckled. "After we debone you all, you're going *straight* to a Mush Station. Gets me hard just thinkin' about it." Lastly the cop gave his own crotch a gratifying squeeze. "In fact, I'm gonna have to corn-hole one'a you'se right here'n now. Any volunteers?" And it was then that the bus fully passed over Tilling.

Now his terror scaled down a notch. *Wow, this is captivating! I'm like a ghost!*

"Okay," Tevi continued. "It'll take you a few minutes to learn how to move around. Best way to get the hang of it is to imagine yourself jumping up in the air, shooting straight up, like Superman."

Tilling didn't get it, but when he did as instructed—

SWOOSH!

—his consciousness shot upward like a surface-to-air missile, and this was the first opportunity he had to look up at the sky.

He gulped in spite of having no throat to gulp with.

The sky was a swarm of churning madness, bearing no semblance to what Tilling for all his life had conceived of as a sky. It was glowing darkly, not blue but the color of blood, and it seemed to *beat* vaguely as if it were indeed blood being pumped by some immense insane heart that couldn't be fully seen. The moon was now a black sickle-shape, and across it streamed streaks of clouds so black they could've been comprised of coal smoke.

And in that impossible scape of blood-red, he saw *things*—things that were *flying*, in the fashion of birds, only these were not birds, for birds were not the size of small airplanes, nor did they possess heads fitted with vulpine fangs, eyes larger than basketballs but otherwise human, and horns like a ram's. One dove downward like a dive bomber, then propelled itself back upward with claws full of what appeared to be entrails. Another flew languidly by with its talons wrapped around a baby with slate-gray skin and diminutive nubs for horns on its forehead. Next, Tilling watched astounded as something like a hot-air balloon floated by. Hanging below the balloon was a long canoe-shaped platform in which men—or things *like* men—ejected screaming naked women whose ear-splitting screams faded as they plummeted. Finally a hugely pregnant woman was pushed out; all of the balloon's crew leaned over the side, grinning as they watched.

It was at this point that Tilling's trajectory upward began to retard, then cease, and next he was plummeting himself. When he looked down he realized he must be miles high, for what he saw below him was a city but unlike any other city he'd ever seen. It seemed limitless and without borders. This high up, it looked like a microcircuit board under a magnifying glass: all straight lines and angles and channels branching out mazelike, and interspersed with all manner of larger geometric shapes which, as his descent brought him closer, turned out to be the tops of skyscrapers, factories, and endless configurations of buildings. Whatever the nature of Tilling's current "being" was, he felt no wind against his face (he *had* no face), and he had no sense of temperature or air pressure. But he could indeed see and also smell, the fact of this latter sense driving home right now as he fell closer and closer to the street where he'd emerged. A variety of stenches *assailed* him, the least of which were the industrial smells coming from myriad smokestacks from factories below. Far worse were the tendrils of separate stenches which reached him. Foremost was organic decomposition like dead things in the sun, or stenches like the stench of an open dumpster behind a butcher's shop or seafood market; and a close second was the undeniable smell of excrement—human or otherwise—as rich as an incoming sea mist. *God Almighty!* he thought, appalled, and he very much wanted to throw up but of course couldn't—he had no stomach at the moment. Next it occurred to him, *I'm a bodiless entity of some kind so...what happens when I hit the pavement?* for he was still falling fast below the blood-red sky, and now he was starting to plummet alongside the tallest skyscrapers which were all miles high. *Damn it, Tevi! Tell me what to do!* his thoughts screamed. He fell past windows but was falling too fast to see anything in them, but from below he could hear a cacophony of screams, shouts, sobbing, ear-splitting machine sounds, and occasional laughter. Finally Tevi's voice returned to him. "This is how you control yourself in Hell—it's with your mind, because that's all you've got over there. Just imagine yourself as, like, a balloon. When you wanna move left, you picture a balloon moving left, and it you wanna move right—do like that. You wanna go up, think of the balloon going up. You'll figure it out—"

Tilling immediately pictured a balloon dropping and thought *Stop!*

His descent halted a few feet from the street. Then he pictured himself moving slowly forward and he began to move forward in actuality.

Each side of the street he was on appeared not terribly different from that of streets in New York, San Francisco, and other big cities: clothing shops, eateries, brownstone-like townhouses with APARTMENTS FOR RENT signs. But the first oddity was this: he immediately noticed dozens if not hundreds of severed penises peppering the street itself and the sidewalks. One old human man hobbled along, then inadvertently stepped on a penis and fell. "Fuckin' dicks!" he complained, waving a cane. "There ought to be a law!" Though many of the penises were human, just as many weren't, reducing the street to a veritable showcase of male genitals from all manner of Hellborn species. Some looked like small gray elephant trunks rolled up, others were multi-pronged or had small humanish heads where the coronas should be. Some looked like sea squirts, centipedes, and tentacles complete with suckers. *Why do they have all these severed penises here?* Tilling thought in rising aggravation. But then he looked up at the street sign, read SEVERED PENIS STREET, and thought, *Oh. That's why...* On the other side of the road Tilling spied a gaunt swollen-faced Imp in one of those orange safety vests walking along with a large white bucket full of severed penises. Every few steps he'd reach in, grab a handful, and then fling them to either side.

"One thing you'll probably see right away are the Bruellenkopfs," Tevi's voice came back. "They're demon-possessed severed human heads that roll around in packs, screaming. They eat the handicapped and homeless bums. It's a trip." And of all the coincidences, at just that moment Tilling heard salvos of high-pitched shrieking, and up ahead he spotted at least a dozen of these severed heads—these Bruellenkopfs—rolling down the street in formation. Tilling watched in horrified fascination as the heads swerved into an alley and clustered around and on top of a demon-hybrid man—apparently homeless—and started eating him alive. Each head took a big bite and then rolled away, giggling. When they were done, in less than a minute—all that remained was a twitching skeleton. Tilling let his consciousness lean forward, and then whatever the vessel was that encapsulated his sentience accelerated away. No, Severed Penis Street wasn't much to Tilling's liking.

The next street—Bianchi Blvd—looked a bit more commonplace; it seemed to be an entertainment district. FIRST RUN! a glittering theater marque read. PARANORMAL NUDIST CAMP MASSACRE! LITTLE CONCENTRATION CAMP ON THE PRAIRIE! TELETUBBIES GO TO HELL!

Doesn't sound like my cup of tea, Tilling thought. He floated past as hastily as he could, but his own morbidity forced him to stop at the next establishment. LIVE SEX! blinked a gaudy sign. *This might be a little more interesting.* For, once, many years ago a friend had taken him to a live-sex club in Manhattan which wasn't half-bad. He utilized his advantage of being sub-corporeal and floated invisibly past the greenish leprous woman selling tickets from a booth. He drifted into a long room fitted with bleachers (filled to capacity, by the way, with Imps, Demons, Zombie, Werewolves, and upscale Humans), that displayed various platforms on which live-sex shows were indeed taking place. But then Tilling saw what they'd left off of the sign out front:

LIVE *TORSO* SEX!

Male torsos were walking around on their stumps, looking for a suitable female torso with which to proceed.

Tilling spied more establishments as he moved on; the area reminded him of Times Square in the '70s. More and more flashing lights and signs promising all manner of debauchery. "Tits, clits, and ice-cold Schlitz!" one door barker announced at one place whose sign read FEMALE CIRCUMCISION CONTEST! and the next place read LIVE DICK DISSECTION with a smaller sign that read HELP WANTED. CORPSE PORN! blared the next marquee, and CADAVER BEAUTY CONTEST! ENTER NOW TO WIN 50 HELLNOTES! under which a line of a dozen rotten women formed; some were rotted in places down to the bone. Tilling, nauseated, had no interest in witnessing such things, but the next establishment gave him reason to pause:

JEFFREY EPSTEIN FUNHOUSE!

What on earth..., Tilling wondered. Even without forethought, his consciousness began to move into the door.

Center-stage stood none other than the naked long-faced, steel-gray-haired finance manager and hedge-fund speculator/con man of such notorious repute. He'd been lashed to a pole—naked, of course—set into the center of a Power Circle filled with pentagrams, planetary symbols, and numerous astrological icons, all of which glowed eerily beneath Epstein's feet. More bleachers faced the spectacle and most spaces were already filled with demonic Dukes, Chevaliers, Tartarean Entrepreneurs, and other well-heeled ticket-holders. The sense of anticipation within grew electric, especially when a Grade One Bio-Wizard levitated across the stage and took his place at what appeared to be an instrument console, but there were precious few gauges and switches here; instead there were candles of various colors and clusters of blinking gemstones. Over the console hung an inverted cross.

Describing the Bio-Wizard himself presented multiple levels of difficulty because this unique Infernal being occupied multiple levels of Nether-Reality. Some of these realities were corporeal, some para-corporeal, and some were amalgamations of both, such that the thing's physicality was hard to observe. If anything, it reminded Tilling of an ancient Samurai warrior, with black planar armor. Nothing even close to a face existed within the helm. Just shifting, illumined static. An orange halo of luminous gas floated above the occult scientist's head, but it was not circular, it replicated the configuration of the upside-down cross overhead.

Tilling floated to an empty seat near the front but then thought *Oops!* when, attempting to sit down, realized he had no buttocks on which to sit.

Applause rose when a horned Conscript in armor of either leather or tanned human skin strode confidently onto the stage, grinning at Mr. Epstein. Epstein himself gibbered and sobbed in the logical fear that something not terribly good was about to happen to him. "Please!" he blubbered. "I'll pay you to let me go! I'm worth half a billion! I'll give you my townhouse in Upper East Side!" The offer was immediately answered by the Conscript's stout hand, producing as if from out of nowhere, a razor-sharp angled Kukri knife, the blade of which was used to slice across Mr. Epstein's forehead, and as a result he screamed high and hard but not nearly as loudly as he bellowed when the Conscript yanked, in a stop-start manner, the financier's scalp off of his shuddering skull. The scalp was then cut loose entirely and tossed to the crowd, leaving the top of Epstein's skull peeled like a bloody orange, whereupon the Conscript began to peel off the child molester's face in a similar manner but downward, until the flap of riven flesh hung off the chin like a bizarre rooster wattle. The majority of space on Epstein's skull was now only blood vessels and intricate musculature. Next the Conscript raised a bucket of powdered salt and emptied it on top of the subject's raw, bleeding head.

The crowd *roared* in approval but not quite loud enough to block out Epstein's bark-like screams.

Next up walked two naked female Broodren, and though they were likely thousands of years old they could've passed for early teens—just the way Jeff liked them. And these Broodren couldn't have been cuter with their barely pubescent breasts, bald pubises, flat pointed ears, and poreless hairless dark slate-green skin. They bowed to the audience then knelt before Mr. Epstein, who was still bellowing non-stop from the salt-treatment. But soon a new tenor accommodated that bellowing, this very much like the ceaseless blare of a truck-horn blown through human vocal cords. The two Broodren giggled as they took to inserting dozens of long sewing needles into the financier's testicles, which one of the ancient children pressured forth by ringing the scrotum with thumb and forefinger. Jeff tensed, twitched, and convulsed on the pole as still more sewing needles made a pair of shiny porcupines out of those famous Epstein family jewels. By the time they were done, Jeff's scrotum could've passed for a modern art masterpiece.

But, alas, there remained the just-as-famous penis itself, which, by now, had understandably shrunk down to the size of a tater tot. That tot, however, was no longer in evidence a moment later when a newly transfected female Flamma-Trooper next took the stage and exhaled a pointed plume of flame—6666 degrees, by the way—directly into Jeff's "junk." The pretty Trooper's veined breasts rose and fell with each fiery gust, and it was at this point that descriptions of Mr. Epstein's vocal protestations began to defy the possibilities of the English language. Lacquered with sweat and grinning with accomplishment, the horned and curvaceous Flamma-Trooper turned to the audience, bowed, then traipsed off amid more applause.

Smoke poured out of the charred hole that had once been the abode of Jeff's felonious cock and balls, the agony having been so intense that his eyeballs had actually popped out of his peeled head. Such treatment, of course, would have ended the life of anyone, but here, in Hell, the Human Damned *could never die*, for their condemnation was eternal. In other words, Jeff, as much as he wanted to, was wholly unable to give up the ghost. He was wholly unable to stop screaming too.

But there was much more pain to be mined from the nervous system of poor Jeff, and this was effected, not by further extremes of physical torture, but by the latest demonstrations of occult science. The lights dimmed and then a spotlight fell on the Bio-Wizard behind his gemological console. The sinister figure then began to murmur, in the Pnakotic language, what was known as an Excruciation Spell, which collected from Mr. Epstein's memory every instance of pain he'd ever experienced in his life as well as all of the pain he'd ever experienced in Hell—including the immediately previous spectacles—and in one wave of the Bio-Wizard's dark hand which produced a single flavescent lance of psychic energy, the famed financier received the opportunity to experience all that pain again, and all at once. Payback, as the saying went, was a bitch. The mauled, skull-faced form of Jeffrey Epstein began to spasmodically convulse so rapidly that his physical form on the pole turned into a manic blur. The man screamed so loud that many spectators had to put in earplugs.

But now was the time for the Bio-Wizard to really strut his stuff. He paused for effect, shifting in and out of full substance, raised his hands as if on the brink of performing a miracle, and then grabbed a glowing console stone and began to turn it as one would turn a knob.

The crowd *Oooh'd* and *Ahhh'd*. The light inside the Power Circle tinted pink and then began to increase in intensity as if the Bio-Wizard were turning up a dimmer knob. This effectively made everything inside the Circle go back in time to just before the beginning of Mr. Epstein's torture session. His scalp, his face, his testicles and his tater-tot penis were totally rejuvenated until he was as intact as he'd been before the show had started.

"Next show starts in fifteen minutes," a demonic voice announced over an intercom.

So the implication was clear. This was how Mr Epstein would spend eternity: being destroyed by torture only to be re-formed so he could be tortured again and again and again, forever and ever.

Fitting as the punishment may have been, it was a bit much for Tilling's milquetoast sensibilities. He urged himself out of there without hesitation.

So this is Hell, he said to himself. *I better start going to church...*

More peep shows, massage parlors, and live sex shows lined the street in even heavier numbers, ornamented by more and more flashing lights. LAST BREATH BOTTLING INC. - WHOLESALERS WELCOME, and DEPARTMENT OF TRANSFIGURATION SURGERY boasted the next sign; the large front window made no secret of what was going on inside. A comely Human woman had been cut in half at the waist, while the bottom half of a Satyr was being surgically attached to the woman. The Satyr's sheathed penis looked donkey-sized. "I can't wait to ass-fuck my useless cheating husband with *this!*" the woman exclaimed. "I'm gonna bust a nut right up in the middle of his shit!" Next, in a row, came FISTING PARLOR, GUT-FUCK PARLOR, and SOUNDING PARLOR. Tilling couldn't imagine what the "sounding" parlor was until a quick peek showed lab-coated technicians with monstrous faces inserting very long dowel rods into the "dick-holes" of several men's penises. In the next window, more Demons in labcoats were using hole-saws to cut one-inch disks out of a variety of people's foreheads, and then they began to insert clusters of things like purple mealworms, baby snakes, and millipedes into the holes. TREPANATION SALON the sign flashed. *Oh, dear,* Tilling thought. *This is not my wheelhouse...* BRAIN LIPOSUCTION! promised the next sign. Tilling shook his non-physical head. *Nope!* He didn't need to look in that window.

He glided farther down the smoking road, appalled yet fascinated. On each corner stood nine-foot-tall Golems made of reeking clay. Next came a street vendor with a wheeled cart. The vendor himself looked like a Human man covered with shelf fungous. "Snacks!

Drinks! Candy!" he announced in a corroded voice. Tilling couldn't help but look down at the seller's wares: Snot Tarts, Phlegmon Drops, Chocolate Covered Dick Knobs, Pussy Lip Gummies. *Nope, nope, nope,* thought Tilling. 2-4-ONE SPECIAL read a plaque over some bags that looked like potato chip bags. TAINT JERKY.

Tilling winced as best he could and moved on, to Vasculitis Blvd. Here the pedestrian traffic thickened, loaded with all manner of Humans, Demons, monsters, and diabolical hybrids. Some beings looked like they were formed with excrement, and many different types of horned beings walked side by side with winged beings. Here was a line of headless nuns, and there a cluster of naked, gray-skinned succubi, all grinning through blood-smeared mouths. Tilling thought of Bosch's *Garden of Earthly Delights* when he espied a pregnant man with buttocks for a head and a pointed cap walking on legs like a goat's. Additionally, this figure brandished an erection and seemed to be in pursuit of a group of small monkeys with female human heads. Just after was a statue of Hideki Tojo, once the pro-war prime minster of Imperial Japan. The statue was pointing to the left, with a sign under his arm that read: DIABLE DE MANIOR - 666 FEET. *Nope,* Tilling thought again and glided right along. A sign in the other direction read HOME CHOPPING NETWORK and then the next: HEXAVISION ARCADE! WATCH WHAT THE LIVING WORLD WATCHES! ONLY 50 HELLNOTES PER HOUR! For whatever reasons, this sign left Tilling in the midst of an intractable state of curiosity, so he floated into the entrance and spotted rows of what appeared to be TV sets, only not the commonplace flat screens of the modern world but old clunky box televisions with small circular screens with wavy lines of static shifting from top to bottom. One screen was showing, of all things, an old episode of the original *Star Trek,* and DeForest Kelly yelling, "Damn it Spock! He's a man, not a machine!" The next screen showed *Squid Game* and the next *Ozark.* Tilling didn't get it. These were popular modern TV shows that aired in the Living World but—

But this was *Hell.*

How could *Hell* possibly show modern TV shows?

They must have some kind really high technology here, Tilling guessed. More bewildered glances showed him more of the same: *Cobra Kai, Mindhunter, Midnight Mass.* These were all shows that Tilling had seen in his own living room, and here they were airing in Hell. *This is absolutely astounding,* Tilling realized. *Tevi wasn't kidding when she said that Hell has evolved right alongside human civilization...*

A blinking sign over the next area read SPORTS BOOK, and along one wall were cashier windows occupied by various women, some demonic, some vampires, and some reanimated cadavers. The wall opposite hosted many more televisions that showed sports games: soccer, basketball, football. Patrons milled about, all clasping tickets of some sort in either their hands or claws. Several tall, winged men stood by, watching intently. Their skin seemed luminous and their eyes could've been hot coals. "God *DAMN* it!" one yelled when a basketball player missed a free throw, but the vocal objection was so loud that it rocked the entire room. "Relax, Moloch," another winged man urged. "It's only a game." "Fuck you only a game! I just lost half a million Hellnotes!" Tilling could only assume that these were Fallen Angels. An Imp in a suit and tie shouted with glee at the next TV, throwing his taloned hands into the air. "I can't believe it! We won!" Tilling—not a fan of sports—took only a cursory glance at the set and saw a team in white jerseys and red pants running maniacally around the field, while the red jerseyed team—clearly the losers—walked off with their heads down. A nearly apoplectic announcer exclaimed, "Who could've predicted this? The last place Washington Football Team has just defeated the World Champion Tampa Bay Buccaneers, 29 to 19!" An old bald Human man next to the Imp griped, "Oh, for shit's sake! *Washington?* What a ripoff!" Tilling would've paid this no mind until he noted something peculiar on the screen. Above the score box in the upper left corner was the date, and it read NOVEMBER 14.

Now that's a bizarre thing, Tilling thought. *I'm certain that today is November 8...*

But before he could contemplate this oddity any further, everything around him seemed to dim as if the blood supply to his brain were being reduced. Warbling, Tevi's voice returned, said "It's time to come back now. Don't be afraid." And the urban hellscape he'd been wandering in disappeared as effectively as if a light switch had been clicked off, and there he was, still bodiless, corkscrewing back through the impossible black tunnel, moving so fast ice seemed to be forming on his psyche. Did he glimpse figures looking at him as he passed, warped faces of persons he'd known? First there came a shrieking so loud he thought his head would split—even though he didn't really *have* a head. Was the shrieking some manifestation of his own screams? Up ahead, as he uncontrollably tossed and turned down the black tunnel, he saw a tiny, fluctuation, a yellowish dot that grew minutely larger, and it occurred to him that he was looking down the wrong end of a telescope. That high-frequency drone—like a hearing test—returned, then the black tunnel stopped and a final scream resounded and there was Tilling lying with his back on the sigil in the basement, gasping like a fish out of water, the candles guttering, and the only sound now was the steady tick of the clock on the shelf.

Am I alive? he thought, but, yes, he had to be. He could feel his heart thumping in his chest, and he could feel the rampant dizziness leftover from his manic spiral up the black tunnel back to this little room in the basement.

It was hard to think. His teeth ground as he struggled to regain his bearings. *That stuff in the pipe, the jaunt... I've just been to Hell and back. It's all true...*

He was so winded he could barely breathe, and when he tried to move he couldn't—he felt pinned down by a hot weight. "Tevi," he croaked. "Where are you?"

"I'm—fuck... I'm right here," she murmured but the gust of words were right at his ear.

Tilling realized then that *she* was the hot weight.

His pants had been pulled down, and Tevi had collapsed on him, her bare legs straddling him. Only now did Tilling feel his cock going limp inside her, and copious semen running out of her. Winded herself, she leaned up over him on her elbows, her bare beautiful breasts right in his face, glazed with sweat.

"For shit's sake, man," she said, grinning down at him. "That might've been the best fuck of my life. Shit..."

"Why the hell am I...like this?" he almost yelled.

She laughed. "You mean, why is your dick in my pussy? Well, because I put it there when you were still on the jaunt." She rolled off of him, still chuckling. "It's just the way it is. The fumes, the incantation, the sigil. It all kind of works on you. Jerry used to say it was the proximity to Hell during a jaunt, even on this side. Doing this ritual makes the wall between this world and that other one very thin. It's like a super aphrodisiac. I couldn't help it. You were just sitting there, I was getting out-of-my-mind horny so—fuck it. I pulled your pants down and banged your brains out." She rolled her eyes in some potent recollection. "You came in me like a fucking fire hose."

Tilled stewed where he lay. "You're telling me I just had sex and don't even remember it?"

She sat up next to him, her nipples still gorged. "Well, yeah, there is that. Sucks for you but—" She shot him a cruel grin. "Not for me."

What an outrage. I just got laid by a woman I'm probably enamored of and I don't remember a bit of it!

"I'll bet it feels like you were there for hours, huh?" she said.

He thought about it. "Actually, yes."

She pointed to the clock on the shelf. It read 12:06.

In a split moment she was up and bending over him, those magnificent breasts hovering. "Pull your pants up," she said. "It's time to get you back upstairs so you can tell me all about your jaunt..."

"The buildings were even harder to comprehend than the red sky." He was reciting his experience in dry monotone. "They had to have been *miles* high. Several years ago I saw the new World Trade Tower but it's nothing compared to the skyscrapers I just saw in the Mephistopolis."

They both sat slouched on the old couch upstairs, Tilling feeling thrilled, comfortable, and thoroughly exhausted at the same time. Before coming back upstairs, Tevi took off the Ambix around Tilling's neck and put it back in the little box marked for him. "If you ever do jaunts on your own, never, and I mean *never* forget to take off your Ambix. If you accidentally went to sleep with it on, you'd be royally fucked up, you'd have non-stop nightmares of Hell. One time Jerry slept with his on and he was a gibbering basket-case for a week."

Tilling didn't want to think of himself as a gibbering basket-case.

Tevi had put her shorts and bikini top back on; naked, she was simply too distracting.

"When I was floating up in the sky," he began, lifting his glass of wine from the coffee table, "I could see what you meant by describing the city as endless."

"And you were in just one tiny place, like one piece of sand on a beach." She stretched her legs out on the table, crossing her ankles. Again, Tilling wondered if she were doing it on purpose; the sight of her tanned legs was getting him going again. "But there's not enough time to go on much of a tour, even if the six minutes equals several hours over there," she went on. "I guess it would take hundreds of years to see the whole place. But let me ask you this: do you think it's all real? Or just hallucination based on the power of suggestion?"

Tilling was surprised by how easy it was to answer. "I'm certain now that my experience was *not* hallucinatory. And I'm shocked by how calmly I'm assessing that truth. There really is an afterlife. There really is a Hell so there—"

"—so there must really be a Heaven too," Tevi continued his sentence. "Which also means there really is a Devil and there really is a God."

That word—*God*—resounded in Tilling's head with a palpable impact. He'd never much considered the prospect before because it struck him as absurd. Now, though?

Shit...

"Makes your head spin, doesn't it?" Tevi said, amusedly.

"Yes, it does."

When she sat up and lit a cigarette, Tilling—a fussbudget—frowned. He was about to ask her to put it out but then almost laughed to himself. *I just smoked a pipe full of satanic drugs, so I guess there's no harm in her smoking a cigarette...*

"So I guess you landed near the street with all the chopped-off dicks on it, right?"

"Severed Penis Street, yes!" Tilling exclaimed. "And I think the next street was full of movie theaters, Bianchi Boulevard, I think."

"Lots of streets in Hell are named after evil Humans. According to Jerry, Bianchi was one of the Hillside Stranglers. There's even a Hitler Street somewhere, and a giant park named after Stalin. Anyway, you landed in the same area that Jerry always landed in, and me too. It's in a section of town called the Boniface District. It's like the part of town where rich residents go for entertainment."

Tilling nodded grimly. "Yes, entertainment, like Jeffrey Epstein's Funhouse and the Gut-Fuck Parlor."

Tevi shrugged. "Well, what do you expect in Hell? Chuck E. Cheese?" She tamped her cigarette out, sipped more wine, then flopped over with the side of her head in Tilling's lap. Tilling tensed momentarily. It almost felt romantic but of course that was nonsense. "And I guess you saw the street vendors and all that shit—"

Tilling's stomach lurched. "Yes, indeed I did. Snot Tarts and Taint Jerky."

"Yuck. What a fucked up place."

Her cheek was pressing right again Tilling's crotch; he needed to become less aware of that; otherwise— "What determines where one enters?" he asked. "What I mean is, is it always that same area? Severed Penis Street and Bianchi? You know about it so you must've seen it."

"Oh, sure, I saw it, and so did Jerry, every time he did a jaunt. That's where we both landed. But why there? Who knows? Jerry thought it had something to do with some inter-dimensional shit; I think he called it super-Copernican intersections. He said Heaven and Hell aren't in parallel dimensions, they're in *perpendicular* ones. You land the same place every time if you start the *invocation* at the same place every time. If we did it from a basement in Pittsburgh instead of *your* basement, we'd land some place else. Don't know the why's and wherefore's. All that matters is it works."

Tilling sat back in the couch. Her warm cheek on his crotch was getting him hard. *Damn it, she'll notice...*

"Jerry got addicted to the place," she said. "I didn't get it. I guess he was more of a perv than I thought. Who'd want to see shit like that? Torture salons, demonic transfusion clinics. Whorehouses in Hell... Holy shit, what could be more fucked up? And Satan built it all, to his exact specifications."

Tilling gritted his teeth as his cock grew harder. *Get your mind off her!* "Addicted, you say? But what would there be to get addicted to in a non-physical state of being?"

"Oh, I'm sure it was just the thrill of it all, seeing all that crazy stuff that no one else gets to see—at least, until they die. Jerry did a *lot* of things in his life, he traveled to a *lot* of different places. I told you, he was an adventurer. *That's* what he got addicted to."

"And what greater adventure could there be than going to Hell and coming back to talk about it?" Tilling summoned all his bravado and gently placed his hand on her side. Feeling her body this close was maddening; it upped his heart rate. Her bare skin around her bikini strap felt delectably warm.

He thought sure that she would comment but that didn't happen.

The harder he tried *not* to focus his thoughts on her, the more his erection filled with blood. *What a problem for an old man to have!* But then the thought hit his brain like a dart. "I'm gonna have to do another jaunt—"

"*Bad* idea!" she snapped. "A really stupid dumb-ass moron idea!"

He used the sudden elevation in discourse as an excuse to slide his hand down over her hot, flat belly. "Why? What's the big deal? Jerry did it a bunch of times—"

"Jerry's a fuckin' vegetable! And that's probably the reason! All that shit in the pipe he smoked is probably what turned him senile!"

Tilling's hand pressed more urgently against her belly. "Advanced age is probably what caused Jerry's cognitive impairment. I'm twenty-five years young than him. And I won't do it that many times."

"Fuck, man! That's what I said when first started popping Vicodins, and the next thing I know I was snorting Fentanyl and blowing guys behind 7-Elevens for ten bucks a pop!"

Without even thinking, he moved his hand up and grabbed her upper arm, excited. "We should do it together!"

"No!"

"Let's do a jaunt at the same time! Now *that* would be an adventure!"

"Fuck no! I told you, I'm never doing it again! Don't ask me why!"

Tilling, in spite of her heated demand, was about to ask why anyway, but then he slammed on his mental brakes. *You're upsetting her, stop it! Stop pissing her off!* "Okay, I'm sorry. I'll never suggest it again. I'm just...so keyed up. It's the most exciting feeling, and it's like nothing I've ever experienced before. But I'll just do it by myself."

"You shouldn't," she murmured in his lap.

Leave it be... Again, without thinking, he moved his hand, this time to cup her left breast. *It's like a hot grapefruit with a bonbon on top*, came the ridiculous simile. In fact, he could feel that "bonbon" hardening under the orange bikini cup. He squeezed slowly and deliberately, to see what she'd say, but again she said nothing. There was nothing in the world he wanted more just then than to fuck her. *She'll want money*, he realized. *But so what? Pay her. I can't expect a young beautiful girl like her to WANT to have sex with an old crumb like me.* He recalled a comedy film from ages ago where a beautiful girl tells an old man, *I don't fuck fossils for free.* He almost laughed right then and there. *That's me. The fossil!*

Even so. Between Tevi's head in his lap, his erection throbbing, and what he'd experienced at midnight, Tilling had never felt more alive...

Yes! I'm the happiest fossil in the world!

Now his hand explored the left breast more intently, then the right. He could swear he felt her nipples pulsing.

"You keep fooling around with those," she said, "there's a price to pay."

"How much?" He kept fondling, each squeeze a wonder.

"And I don't mean money. Nympho, slut, sex maniac, whatever you want to call it, that's me. If you make me horny, I will ride you like one of those mechanical bulls."

"Oh, yeah?"

"If you turn me on, there's no turning me off till my nut is *busted*. Just so you know. You've been warned."

Oh, for pity's sake! Be demonstrative for once in your life! he thought then pushed her head off his lap, stood up quite abruptly, and next— as much as it surprised him—was yanking off her cut-offs, practically turning her upside down. "God damn!" she giggled. "Rough me up, why don't you—"

Tilling unceremoniously pulled his pants down, reseated himself on the couch, then pulled Tevi right next to him. He untied her top, slipped it off. She squealed when he lifted her up by her hips, then lowered her groin right down on his crotch, which slammed his cock into her without so much as a fidget.

What a luxury, he thought.

She was already drenched inside. He could've swooned at the feel of his erection encased in her sex. He slowly thrust himself in and out; he could feel her arms and legs tensing, then he put his arms around her and pulled her bare breasts directly into his face. *What a wonderful creature she is*, he thought, heart racing. *And what a perfect vision...* Tilling thought that if he didn't go to Heaven when he died, this—this vision right in front of him—was good enough. It was all the Heaven he would ever need.

Tevi was already breathing hard, she was squirming, her movements urgent if not frantic. *Don't come in two seconds, you old fud!* he tried to order himself but he wasn't quite sure if he could manage that. His mouth attached to her nipple and began to suck hard, then harder till she squealed. But then, as mind-bogglingly intense as the experience was, those mental brakes slammed on again—

What a minute! he thought and then barked the words aloud: "Wait a minute! Damn it, how could I forget?" and his hard upward thrusts stopped abruptly.

The reaction on her face looked crazy. "What the FUCK? Don't stop!"

But Tilling stopped, his mind instantly aswarm with a previous observation. "There's something I forgot to tell you."

"Really? *Now?* Balls deep in my pussy and my tits in your face?"

He lifted her off him and dropped her just aside. She frowned agape at his cock, which was harder than it had been in twenty years and throbbed ludicrously in the air, his balls bunched up.

"Listen, this is incredible. It was right at the end of my jaunt!" he explained in exhausted excitement. "I don't remember the name of the street but there was a big statue of Tojo—"

"Who?"

"He was the Japanese—never mind. But there was this place called the Hexavision Arcade. Did you happen to see that when you did your jaunt?"

"No, but I know what Hexavision is. It's Hell's version of TV. According to Jerry, there are no radio or television signals in Hell, but they have this other stuff call Hell-Flux. It's sort of like electro-magnetic signals."

"Okay, then that makes sense," Tilling calculated. "There were whole banks of these weird televisions, showing TV shows. And a little ways on there was this other place. One time I went to a teacher's convention in Vegas and I saw my first casino. Have you ever been to a casino?"

Tevil frowned. "I'm an American Indian. My tribe *owns* casinos. My first *jobs* were in casinos. That's like asking an Eskimo if they've ever seen ice."

"Okay. So then you might know what I'm talking about. There was this place in the back called Sports Book or something, and there were a lot more TVs—"

"Yeah, every casino has a place like that," Tevi said. "It's where people can bet on horse races, NASCAR, baseball games, that kind of shit."

"Right!" Tilling exclaimed. "And that's what people were doing here—"

Tevi scratched her head. "I never saw that, and Jerry never mentioned it. So they were betting on horse races in *Hell?* I'd hate to see what the horses look like."

"That's just it. They weren't betting on anything in Hell, they were betting on sports games taking place *here.*"

Her brow furrowed. "You mean *here*, as in our world, the Living World?"

"Yes! It was the weirdest thing. First, they had TV shows that air here on cable, and then they had this Sports Book place, and you could see on the TVs various pro football games."

Tevi paused, thinking. "That's incredible. I know there's a lot of occult technology in Hell, and Jerry said some of the stuff is getting very advanced but...*earthly television?* They must've invented some kind of wacky antenna that somehow picks up *our* TV broadcasts."

"That has to be it!" Tilling said. "And that's what people were betting on. People in Hell, betting on football games *here!* And there was one game—Washington, I think, and they were playing a team I think I've heard of...the Buccaneers?"

Another harsh frown from Tevi. "I guess you don't know shit about sports, huh?"

"Well, no, not at all."

"The Buccaneers are the *home team*. They won the fuckin' Super Bowl last year."

"Okay, yes, yes, the announcer said that, that they were the current world champions, but they just lost to this other team, Washington, and it was a big surprise because evidently Washington's not very good—"

"Washington sucks dog dicks," Tevi elaborated. "Some high school teams could probably beat them. But you're telling me they *beat* the Bucs?"

"Yes, 29-19."

A drawn out pause. "They haven't even *played* the Bucs this year." She jumped up and grabbed a newspaper off a table by the front door, and began flipping through it.

"That's what I wanted to tell you," Tilling went on. "When the game was over, I looked up at the score and they showed the date: November 14th."

Tevi looked up from the paper and gaped at him. "Yesterday was November 8th—"

"Exactly..."

Tevi went back to rummaging through the newspaper, more frantic this time. Then— "Fuck. Washington plays the Bucs next Sunday. November 14th..."

Tilling stared at her, not even seeing her stunning nude body. "How...could that be possible? Hell exists...in the *future?*"

"How do you like that conniving old fuck?" Tevi growled, rage in her eyes. Now she began to stalk circles around the room, shaking her head in an attitude of genuine scorn. "*That's* how the motherfucker made all his money. Never peeped a word of it to me, the greedy fuck, and after all the shit I did for him. I don't think I've ever been as pissed off as I am right now."

Tilling sat bewildered. "I don't understand what you mean."

"Jerry knows a *lot* about Hell. He jaunted there a huge number of times, over decades," she said, still walking nude circles around the living room. "One thing he told me a long time ago was that Hell exists on a different time-line than the Living World. It's six days in the future..."

Oh, my— Tilling's eyes bloomed. Now he was starting to understand.

"But he never told me about this Sports Book place," she continued to sputter. "And he never mentioned a word about Hell discovering the technology to intercept television signals from the Living World. Of course not! He wanted to keep the secret to himself! Hoard all that money for *himself!*"

"The secret being," Tilling plainly assumed, "he would go to Hell, see what sports teams won *six days before* the games even occurred here. Then he'd place his bets and win every time. God only knows how much money he made."

Tevi's rage had finally burned out all her energy. She just stood there now, tears at the corners of her eyes. "How could somebody be *that* greedy? He knew I didn't have shit, and the whole time he was paying me chump change while he must've had a mountain of loot somewhere. All this time I thought I meant something to him. But I wasn't anything to him except a burned out Indian chick who'd mop his floors, clean his toilets, and suck his dick every Friday fuckin' night." She staggered back to the couch, sat back down, and began to sob outright.

Life can be very complicated, I suppose, Tilling thought. *Too many monkey wrenches that I've never been cut out for.* He pulled his pants back up, feeling useless. He couldn't think of anything to say to make her feel better. "Love of money is the root of all evil, they say in the Bible somewhere. And deceit wears many faces. But it seems that Jerry, in his all consuming greed and falsehood, has left the door wide open for us."

Tevi gulped and sniffled, then looked up at him with a tear-streaked face.

"I'm quite sure we're both about to become very very rich," Tilling said, smiling at her.

Tilling was surprised that he'd survived the night. He and Tevi had gone to bed together, whereupon she'd sexually marauded him, several times in a row, leaving him scarcely able to move. *Good God, she damn near fucked me to death...* But what retired man in his '60s would complain about that? That night he'd slept, indeed, like the dead, remembering only blank dreams and some ethereal excitement that had to be subconsciously tethered to their newfound considerations regarding the potential of the "Sports Book." Tilling had wakened in the late morning, to find his heart racing. It was Tevi who'd roused him from slumber, by expertly soliciting his cock with her mouth. Aching all over and flattened by exhaustion, he felt certain that yet another orgasm on his part was out of the question... until he was gasping a moment later and filling her mouth with his senior-citizen sperm. In a rare use of profanity, he thought, *You've gotta be fucking shitting me! Men my age aren't supposed to be able to COME so many times, for fuck's sake!*

Energized, she dashed to the shower, then pulled her scant clothes back on right in front of him. *What a jewel. What a beautiful beautiful woman. How on earth did she wind up in MY bed?*

She pulled out some crumpled cash from her pants pocket and

frantically counted it. "Fuck! I only have sixty bucks! We need money to *bet*, man! How much have you got on you?"

Tilling thought he could hear his bones creak when he got up, pulled on a robe, and consulted his closet. He avoided the nuisance of going to the bank when he could help it, which was why he always kept considerable cash on hand. This he hid in the pocket of an old sports jacket. When he reemerged, he gave Tevi a stack of cash. "Here's how much I trust you, Tevi—this is five thousand dollars. Many girls would disappear with it but I'm relying on my judgment that you won't. Take a cab to the Tampa casino right now and bet it all on Washington. Not if, but *when* we win, we'll split the take fifty-fifty."

"Fuck, yeah!" She fanned the cash out; her eyes bulged. "Shit! This'll be a killing! But…are you sure about the final score?"

Tilling re-saw it in his mind. "29 to 19, Washington. I'm sure."

"So you mean there's no chance you might even be a little teensy bit wrong? Not 28 to 19? Not 29 to 18, or anything like that? Because if you're certain, I'll bet it all on the points-pyramid. It's a way to bet on the *exact* score, and the odds are fuckin' *huge*. But you gotta be *absolutely sure…*"

Tilling made no hesitation when he said, "Bet it all on the points pyramid, Tevi."

Her cheeks were pink with exhilaration when she called a cab. "You should come too," she said. "It'll be a blast."

"No, I'm afraid casinos are little too fast lane for me. I'll leave you to it," he said, but then it occurred to him to add, "And I'm sure I don't need to implore the cruciality of fidelity in this matter."

"*What?*" she winced.

"You mustn't tell *anyone* about *any* of this."

Tevi laughed out loud. "Don't worry, I won't tell anyone. And who would believe it anyway? We're getting inside sports tips from *Hell?*" She stood up on tiptoes, put her arms around him and gave him the lewdest of kisses. "I'll be back later!" and then she zipped out of the room.

My God, Tilling thought, his spirits nearly adrift. *I think I very well might be in love…*

* * * *

Tilling dawdled the afternoon away; he truly believed he would be rich from this impossible happenstance and he was surprised by how easily he'd conformed to it. How could he not? *I went to Hell, and came back. It was not hallucination, psychosis, or delusion. It's REAL.* If someone had told him a week ago that this would happen, he'd dismiss them as utterly insane. He'd been to Hell and back, and he was going again. It seemed as though he'd lived his entire life with a gaping hole in it, but now Tevi and *this* was filling that hole and then some.

He looked back at the set of drawers in the closet and inspected the previously unexamined third drawer. More old hardcover books in fair condition, but these were in English. *Esoteric Philiology and other Anti-Axiomatic Sciences*, one read, and Tilling laughed out loud. *What gobbledygook!* Then *The History Phasmatology* by someone named Abney in 1812. Tilling had never heard the word "phasmatology" and he doubted if it really even existed. Another, *The Teachings of Etherea & Transmigration* by Osthanes Magus. Tilling flipped through some of the old Black Letter typeface and couldn't imagine anything more unreadable. Finally, *What have we here?* A magazine lay at the bottom of the drawer that promised to be anything but boring: an issue of *Penthouse Magazine* from 1973 boasting a staggeringly bosomed Pet of the Month named Avril Lund. The discovery presented a blast from the past; Tilling grinned, broadly flipping through the pages and unfolding the center. He'd shoplifted this same issue at the age of fourteen.

"Here are your receipts," Tevi said upon returning to Tilling's house in the early evening. She gave him the paper tickets that were proof that she'd bet all the money on the exact final score.

"*Our* receipts," he corrected her and placed them on the coffee table.

"It'll be over a hundred grand if we win," she added, pouring herself some wine in a paper cup.

"*When* we win, Tevi, *When*." He smiled at her. "First it was me who was the doubting Thomas. *You* now? We've *both* experienced it directly. We *both* know it's real."

"Yeah, I know. It's just...hard for me to think of myself as being rich, you know. I'm too used to being piss poor."

"All that changes as of next Sunday. You'll never be poor again."

She sat as if in a smiling trance. "I'll be able to get a car. I'll be able to hire a lawyer and get custody back on my kid. I'll finally be able to get a decent place to live—"

"Or you can live here," Tilling hastened, "with your child, of course. I won't get in the way. And once our fortune grows, which it undoubtedly will, we'll get a better place, a house on the water, perhaps, or for that matter, anywhere. We can live anywhere you want."

She smiled at him with narrowed eyes. "It sure sounds like you got plans, hmm?"

"I certainly do," he said. By now he knew that he was in love with her. When he'd more directly considered their age difference, that could present a problem. But still...

He loved her.

That had to be what this was; he'd never felt this way about anyone. *Don't push her in a corner,* he realized. *She can do whatever she wants...* "And if it turns out that my plans and your plans have insufficient common ground, then fine. I'll see to it that we're always friends."

She came over to him, rose again on her tip toes, and kissed him. It was a habit he was starting to get used to. "I already know that we have plenty of common ground," she said. "And I already know you can give me more cock than I can stand—"

"Do you now?" he replied heartily. *So what if she's exaggerating? A little...* He wanted to laugh out loud, he was so exuberant.

Her breasts flattened against him; he could feel her heart fluttering. "So when do you want to do the next jaunt?"

He slid his hands up her hips, as if molding her. "Tonight, of course. There's no reason no to."

The radiance in her eyes stopped down a bit. "Why so soon? Why not wait a while? Don't be like Jerry and get hooked on it. If you do this shit a lot, it'll fuck up your head.."

He hugged her. "I think I'm a bit more prudent than *Jerry.* This isn't something I plan on doing very often—"

"Good."

"—and I am aware there's an element of danger. Unknown drugs. Invocations. The sheer shock of actually seeing Hell. But why not strike when the iron is hot? This time I'll go immediately to the Sports Book, memorize as much as I have time for, and then we'll be set for a long time. Doesn't that sound like a good idea to you?"

"Yeah, I guess it does. But we have to wait till midnight—" She began urging him toward the bedroom. "I'll find something for us to do until then..."

At about ten before midnight Tilling and Tevi were getting prepared in the basement "chancel." Tevi stripped nude as she had last time, leaving Tilling unable to avert his eyes from her bosom as she placed his Ambix around his neck. The peculiar stone in the pendant seemed to give off a confident vibe. *I'm about to go to Hell again,* he thought in the flickering candlelight, and he had no trepidations. In fact he was looking forward to it.

"The reason I'll never do another jaunt myself," Tevi said, "is because—"

"Oh, don't tell me. It's none of my business. I'm sorry for pressuring you on the point earlier."

"It's no big deal, really." She bent over to place the bronze censer in the sigil's center and began to light the cloves. "You need to know because I suppose it could happen to you."

"'It' being...what, exactly?" He was involuntarily painting her with his gaze, her flawless breasts depending, her perfect rump jutting. The candlelight made her silhouette on the wall shift like a lewd ghost.

"During my first and only jaunt," she said, finally standing back up, "I was floating down the street with the statue of the Japanese guy. And I heard screaming coming from a big brick building. I looked through a gap in the bricks because—I don't know—there seemed something familiar about the scream in some way I couldn't really figure. Then I noticed the sign that read Agonocity Station. This is where Hell gets most of its standard domestic energy. You plug in a hair dryer here, it runs on electricity. Plug one in there, it runs on *Agonicty*."

"In other words," Tilling attempted, "this Hellbound energy is produced by some process that involves—"

"Pain," Tevi said, nodding. "Excruciating *agony*. They do it by cutting off the top of your skull and sinking things like electrode-nails right into the pain-centers of your brain. Then a Power Technician—usually a Troll or an Imp—tortures the living shit out of you, usually with boiling water from a hose. Then all the pain you feel is transferred from your brain to a big power converter and gets pumped into the grid. Since the Human Damned can't die in Hell, the torture goes on forever."

Tilling's frail sensitivities caused him to shudder at the implication. "But...what does that have to do with your decision never to jaunt again? Certainly there are worse things to witness in Hell."

"Sure, but when I looked into the Station I saw that it was my *father* they were torturing." Tevi stood blank-faced, then took a deep breath. "My father had his flaws but he was a good person who spent his whole life doing things for other people. It isn't right that he should've gone to Hell when he died. He'll be hooked up to that fuckin' machine for a thousand years, and when the thousand years are over, he'll start on the *next* thousand. It must be my karma or something. Of all the people I could've run into in Hell, and I see my *father*, the only person in my whole damn family who was any good."

Tilling gulped and blinked into the stiff silence that followed. *What could I possibly say that would be of any use to her?*

She seemed to pull her thoughts out of the grim recollection. "So anyway, that's why I told you, so you'd be prepared in case the same thing happens to you. Fuck. Nobody wants to think their dead loved ones are in Hell—but you never know."

Tilling chose not to contemplate the prospect.

He heard the clock ticking. Tevi came around behind him,

guided him toward the edge of the sigil, and urged him to sit down. "It's time," she said in the softest voice. Then she sat down across from him, picked up her cellphone, and began to play the recording of the invocation which solicited the favor of Lucifer—

Tilling soared through foul air beneath the beating, churning, blood-red sky, feeling invulnerable within the invisible sphere of whatever power it was that encapsulated his soul and allowed him to move unseen in the midst of Hell. He knew he could feel himself grinning even without a physical mouth, and seeing without eyes but seeing all the same, beholding the horrific and the spectacular and the impossible. He allowed himself to fall after a moment, then used his imagination to picture him landing softly on the chaotic street below, just as he had yesterday. First, he remembered the sign APARTMENTS FOR RENT along with its accommodating tenement. There were severed heads in the window sills as well as flower pots which sported nothing at all like flowers. Instead there were black, thorned stems topped by things that looked like fingers, toes, ears, and even lips. One window was belching flames; Tilling could see figures moving about in the conflagration. Flaming Demonic babies were tossed out the window only to be snatched right up by more nameless flying things that picked them apart with gusto. Eventually a vehicle sort of like a fire truck arrived, siren wailing, and then Trolls in raincoats and helmets wielded several fire hoses and then aimed the spray directly into any open window. Of course it wasn't water but gasoline or turpentine. In seconds the entire building was engulfed in fire amid cannonades of screams. *Jeez,* Tilling thought. *That's some system they've got here.*

He shook off the images and floated onward, once again on none other than SEVERED PENIS STREET and casting intermittent glances down at the things for which the street was named. *Damn! That's a lot of severed penises!*

"Remember," Tevi's voice fluttered in his head. "You can hear me but I can't hear you. Be fuckin' careful, and don't dick around. Just get to the Sports Book fast and start memorizing any scores you see on the TVs."

Yes, ma'am, he thought. He breezed farther down the road, flinching at quadraphonic screams, cackles, and cacodaemonical laughter. Pedestrians moved down the sidewalk as if without a care in the world, be they Demons, Hybrids, Ghouls, Trolls, etc. And on every corner stood a sentinel of some sort: Golem, Usher, Annelok. Tilling floated past them, and in some cases *through* them, catching atrocious glimpses of their thoughts. Across from the Home Chopping Network, he spied the familiar sign DIABLE DE MANIOR and turned left. *I'm looking for the Hexavision Arcade,* he reminded himself and knew that he was on the right track. Around the corner stood a theater he'd missed on his first trip, and the marquee flashed a double-feature: DON'T MISS THE PREMIER! BOYS-R-US & PEDERASTY PARADISE! But next came something he hadn't noticed before, a blue sign with white letters and a yellow pentagram: PALL-MART. *I've GOT to check this out!* and he used his thoughts to veer into bustling department store. Demons, Trolls, and Humans alike occupied the customary rows of cashier stations, while an even greater variety of Hierarchs, Corrupted Nobility, Wizards and Succubi, Conscript Officers, and Hybrids perused the store's aisles, pushing shopping carts made of bones. Overhead muzak seemed to be the dismal moans of persons being slowly tortured.

Tilling's venture wouldn't last long. First he passed the Women's Undergarment section which sported frilly Virgin Dick Skin panties and sassy bras made from Nether-Ox Tongues (still alive) and Werewolf hands. One horned, yellow-skinned Duchess seemed very interested in the stoles, not stoles made from mink but from lengths of connected public patches. Jewelry boasted bracelets and earrings fitted with gallstones and kidney stones and dried scabs. *Do the denizens of this place actually PAY for such stuff?* Tilling wondered. He breezed down the Garden and Patio section next; instead of 50 lb. bags of topsoil, they were selling 66 lb. bags grave dirt from the Valley of Siddom. A number of potted plants were displayed off to one side, particularly Utero-Gourds (some pregnant, some not) Spitunias whose pus-colored blossoms seemed to revel in expectorating on shoppers, and then there was a fragrant variety of Eyeball-Roses.

Boxes of bone meal from the Haas Emaciation Camps were on sale in a One For The Price Of Six special. Home Improvement hosted discount autopsy saws, peritoneal-drains, and "Header" drills, not that Tilling knew what *that* was. Next came Kitchen Electronics where one could find anything from a Baby Microwave to a Vaginal Aspirator to a Scrotum Pump. Tilling was about to leave but then he spotted the TOYS section. *This I can't resist...*

Hellish mothers followed their squalling children through aisles piled high with infernal toys. Here were some Bugger-Me-Elmo dolls, and then a Suzy Homewrecker Playset which consisted of a doll house in which the titular Suzy cheated on her husband, abused her children, and performed oral sex on dirty drug dealers in exchange for opioids. The next was the Easy Bake Crematorium: happy toddlers were incinerating their parents on the cover art; next, Barbie's Dream Date Set, where an elegant as always Barbie could choose her next beau but there was no expected Ken doll. Instead there was serial killer Richard Ramirez the Night Stalker, Jack the Ripper, and Albert DeSalvo the Boston Strangler. Here was a Retch-a-Sketch and some Rock 'Em-Rape 'Em Robots. Most interesting was the Pikachu Cannibal Corral. And last but not least was the Chatty Lilith doll. A Zombie attendant, with a face completely rotted off, demonstrated the coveted doll before a drove of monstrous children. A cord on the back of the Raggedy-Ann-like head was pulled and then Sally began to talk in a cute little doll-voice: "I hate you!" and "I'm gonna suck your father's cock and then cut it off and put it in my pussy!" and "I'm gonna give your mommy an abortion with an SS bayonet! Glory be to Satan!"

Tilling left the store posthaste.

And Jerry got ADDICTED to coming here? he thought. *Well, he can have it...*

In another moment, there it was: HEXAVISION ARCADE! Tilling mentally nudged himself inside.

Right up front came the standard TV shows he'd noticed yesterday: current Netflix shows and other cable programs and— wouldn't you know it? Fox News. *Tevi's right*, Tilling reflected. *The technology in Hell is incredible—to be able to intercept television signals from another dimension!* And it was time for him and Tevi to really cash in. Tilling drifted immediately to the ESPN scoreboard for the Monday night game on November 15th: the 49ers had just defeated the Rams. This Tilling committed to memory and then did the same with several basketball games. Even better, another TV, this one showing finance news, indicated that the S&P went up .39% to 4700.90, a very easy final number to memorize. *We'll be able to make a fortune on that alone!* he realized.

Trying to memorize more games was unnecessary and might only jumble his memory. He drifted back out of the arcade. A blinking sign read THE BUNG-HOLE and below it a plaque: DANCE CONTEST. So it was a dance club of some sort? Tilling floated in and glimpsed barely visible figures in monstrous shapes slowly dancing in what appeared to be black light. They were not dancing to music, however, but to the strangest clicking noise turned way up in volume and dubbed over and over again at the same time, until Tilling realized what it was: an over-sampling of death-rattles. Next came a row of booths not unlike telephone booths where another sign read CADAVER CANOODLING! ONLY 10 HELLPENNIES PER MINUTE! Tilling couldn't believe his incorporeal eyes: denizens of Hell were paying to squeeze into the booths and "make out" with female corpses.

"Step right up, folks!" announced a man with all his skin peeled off; he stood in front of a mobile vending cart of the kind often used by enterprising persons selling hotdogs, hamburgers, etc., on the street. The lipless face barked, "Get your piping hot Shit-Fish fresh out of the National Waste Water Reservoir! That's right, folks! I said Shit-Fish! It's better than salmon and better than cod, and you can't get that here anyway! So step right up! Limited supply! Cooked to order! Broiled, fried, or poached!" One man in a business suit and a bivalved head came forward: "I'll take a Shit-Fish! Poached!" "Comin' right up, bub," said the solicitor. He stepped behind the cart where a counter displayed a broiler, a deep-fryer, and—

What on earth is she doing there? Tilling wondered, stupefied.

Sitting right next to the deep fryer was a shapely nude Human woman, only there was a metal collar around her neck, and she was chained to the cart. "Fuck," she swore. "Not another one..." The proprietor took a malformed brown fish out of a box, then jammed a skewer through it. "Spread 'em toots," he said to the collared woman. "You know the drill." Disgusted, the woman leaned back and widely spread her legs, displaying a gaping vaginal inlet into which the skinned man inserted the fish. Then the woman clapped her legs closed. "Five minutes, mister," he said to the split-headed man in the suit.

The madness here was beginning to dizzy Tilling. All there was left to do now was wait until the incantation timed out, whereupon he would be pulled back to his physical body. And no sooner had he thought of it—

"Get ready," Tevi's bodiless voice informed him.

Back into the black tunnel he was sucked, spinning round and round like something in a food processor—only this was his spirit. He felt as though he were melting and being whipped like taffy. The corkscrew's velocity trebled every second, until Tilling feared his brains might be sucked right out of his ears, but then he remembered he *had* no ears. Were there dim faces looking at him as he traveled back, likenesses pressed forward out of obsidian blackness? Loved ones? Relatives? His dead parents? Tilling couldn't tell and really didn't want to know. Now, just as before, whatever it was that confined his spirit began to spasm like a fibrillating heart, as he noticed the lit dot at the end getting bigger and bigger, and then—

WHAM!

Just more blackness.

Eventually Tilling's consciousness arose like something lurching out of a tar-pit. Though he understood that the time between the start of the ritual and its end was only really six minutes, this felt *much much* longer. His excitement tried to burst forth—he remembered the scores and stock information from the Arcade in perfect clarity—but—

Something was bogging him down.

He expected to see Tevi, in her stunning nudity, smiling down at him from her place on the sigil's edge, the candles flickering and licking at shadows on the wall.

But there was none of that. Tilling tried to get up, to reach out, to say something, but all he could do was open his eyes. He could see and hear but he couldn't move...

What the Hell?

"Fuck," came a female grunt. "Yeah, harder, just like that. Come in me hard..."

It was Tevi's voice, and when he looked up, he did not recognize where he was. It was just a drab room with almost nothing in it, sunlight blaring from a single window with nondescript curtains. A television—turned off—had been mounted high in a corner, like in a hospital room. In fact, it took him till then to realize that he was lying in a bed in something like a hospital room.

His eyes flicked forward. *I'm sure I heard Tevi,* he thought and, yes, there she was, barely visibly herself. Straight ahead, a man stood with his pants half down, his back toward Tilling; he was copulating frenetically, pounding his groin between Tevi's tanned and widely spread legs. She was sitting on a dresser, her knees jacked up to her shoulders—all the while her suitor continued to slam himself into her loins.

"Aw, fuck—yeah. Just like that," Tevi's voice uttered as her climax passed. "Knock me the fuck up..."

A few more strokes, then the denouement. The man pulled his pants up and chuckled. "If you get pregnant, I will personally cut the baby's head off and suck all its blood out of its neck. Then I'll fuck the remains..."

"I love it when you talk romantic like that! I gets me *so hot!*"

But now Tilling was nearly drowning on his gags, hacking in outrage, choking in unbridled horror. Recognizing the "man's" voice was easy—it was his own voice.

"Oh, look! Our friend's finally awake!" Tevi hopped off the dresser and pulled down her short jean skirt just as a sizeable dollop of sperm slid down her thigh.

And the man finally turned around.

Oh my God! God DAMN them!

It was Tilling himself who turned around and looked at him.

"Ah, Professor Tilling, what a pleasure to meet you. I very much appreciate the use of your body—mine was no good anymore...but of course you're finding that out for yourself right this moment. And what I'm *most* grateful for is the serviceability of your cock. It still works quite well for someone your age, and you can rest assured, I'll be sticking it in our little Tevi's pussy every chance I get."

Tevi opened the door, on the other side of which was a plaque: ORNE, J. Out in the hallway, a comely nurse walked by pushing a med cart. Several old people shuffled along in the opposite direction, either with walkers or canes, and then came an ancient woman in a wheelchair.

"Looks like my acting performance was pretty fuckin' good," Tevi said. "I knew all about the Sports Book and everything else. Jerry was worn out, so it was my job to find him a new body."

"And a job she performed with the utmost proficiency," said the other man. "And by the time I wear *this* body out, she'll simply find me another one."

Tevi grinned down at Tilling. "Can you believe it? This boring old fuck was falling in love with me. Isn't that a riot?"

"Now, now, Tevi," the man in Tilling's body said. He came over behind her, reached around, and squeezed her monumental breasts. "Have some consideration for the man's feelings."

Tevi's sick grin glared down. "I should sit on his face and smother the arrogant piece of shit."

"No, no, my love. It's best we leave the professor be, and let him experience death as slowly as possible."

Tevi stepped closer; she wiped some semen off her thigh and smeared it over Tilling's lips. "There. How's your own cum taste, fuckhead?"

"Women. Absolutely treacherous, aren't they? Absolutely *abominable*."

Tilling noticed that the impostor was wearing one of the pendants that Tevi had called an Ambix, then he looked down at his convalescent gown and was just able to see that he had one on too.

"You're wearing Jerry's old Ambix, and he's wearing yours," Tevi said. "The switch was easy."

"The transposition couldn't have worked more perfectly. Just as the Pnakotic texts assured."

The attractive nurse stuck her head in. "Sorry, folks. Visiting hours are over. I'm afraid you'll have to say goodnight to Mr. Orne."

The face once belonging to Tilling smiled grandly. "Indeed, Mr. Orne. We bid you a *very* good night."

When the nurse departed Tevi spat into Tilling's agape mouth, which, for the life of him, he couldn't close. "Yeah, *Jerry*. Have a good night." She pulled up her top and flashed her breasts. "You can think about these every time you jerk off... Oh, wait a minute! You *can't* jerk off! You're paralyzed!"

Tevi and her cohort left the room, laughing.

Tilling swallowed Tevi's spit out of no recourse, then he stared up at the ceiling, and that's about all he would ever be able to do ever again.

THE NIGHT-SITTER

Jessica would discover the entails of the entire matter only when the matter had ended. But what it began with were the SD cards—

—and what she'd seen on them, what they'd done to that woman's head.

The client's name was Roulet, Edmund Roulet. She'd met him one night web-camming; hence, the reason she thought of him as a "client," though nothing sexual had ever transpired between them. He hadn't asked for a show, or for her to masturbate with any one of her toys. No dirty talk, no "Have you been a bad boy?" He hadn't even jerked off. Instead, he'd only talked to her for a few moments—"Ah, I see from your profile that you're from Florida, so am I."—"Really? Two years of college and a CNA certificate? Impressive."—"Oh, no car? But you do have a driver's license—that's great." He was feeling around for something. Why would a webcam enthusiast care about her education and her driver's license?

He'd turned his own cam on so she could see his face, and this Mr. Roulet's face didn't really reflect the face of a cam-site denizen. He could've been a retired college professor: white hair a bit disheveled, bald spot, spectacles, and a white beard to which the attention of some scissors would be a service. But there was no look of the perv about him, nothing semblant of the typified Dirty Old Man.

"What do you want to see?" she asked. "I like you, let me give you an eye-party," this, of course, because webcamming paid by the minute. "Wanna pussy-show? Around the World? I've got some *big* toys too. I can even fist myself."

But none of this would do. Mr. Roulet had another motive for being on Jessica's link, and what it boiled down to was this: "I'd like to offer you a job, Jessica, a night job, which should present no problem since most cam-girls are nocturnal."

A *night* job? "I'm listening," she said, suspicious.

"I'll pay $500 a night for you to house-sit for me, every night, from dusk till dawn. I offer free room and board as well, if you'd prefer. The only additional duties will be to take out the garbage, retrieve my mail, and run errands for me in the car."

I don't know, Jessica thought. "Did you mean $500 a week?"

"No, no. Per night. I'll have an auxiliary bank account you'll have ATM access to, or I can transfer your pay each night to your own bank account, a recharge card, Paypal, whatever you'd prefer."

She put it point-blank. "It sounds too good to be true, Edmund."

"Please, if you will. Mr. Roulet. And please know that this is not in anyway a sexual proposition—"

Yeah, right, she thought, not that sex would've been any obstacle. Jessica, by the way, was very inclined to transactional arrangements.

"—in fact, you'll very rarely even see me," his pixelated image went on. "I merely want an attractive young woman to sit up at night while I'm asleep." He paused, typing something. "Tell you what. I'll send my address to your profile contact, and how about this?"

The little counter at the bottom of the screen registered only two minutes so far. The site fee was two dollars per minute, but she only got half of that, and there was her total earned so far, showing on the screen: $2.00. *This has got to be pure bullshit*, she reasoned, but then more numerals appeared on screen: TIP: $500.00

"I've just sent you a $500 tip," he went on. "I'll expect you at noon. Take a cab or have a friend drop you off, whatever. And if I don't see you tomorrow, I'll take it that you simply don't want the job, but you may keep the tip with my compliments."

"Uh," she said. "Wow."

He showed her a big, genuine smile. "It's been a distinct pleasure talking to you, Jessica, and I do hope I shall see you tomorrow. So until then, or if not, I bid you a very good night."

Mr. Roulet signed off.

All that anyone had ever deduced about Mr. Roulet was that he was something of a sybaritic recluse, this judged by the always-full recycle bin of very expensive Scotch bottles and steady deliveries from gourmet restaurants. He lived unknown and to himself; in fact, he hadn't been seen by any neighbors for quite some time. The constant presence of a new luxury sedan in his driveway only reinforced the consensus that he was a man of private wealth in spite of the incongruence of the physical state of his old eyesore of a house and untended yard. Neighbors regularly spied empty bottles of Macallan 21 Year Old Fine, Glenmorangie Quarter Century, and Glenfiddich 30, all hundreds per bottle. The proprietor of the nearest liquor store claimed that every two weeks an attractive woman driving Roulet's sedan would purchase one bottle of Remy Martin Louis XIII cognac for $2800.

So. The never-seen Mr. Roulet had something of a drinking problem to accentuate his agoraphobia.

He did, however, insist on the constant employment of a live-in house attendant/night-sitter, who was always a young woman of provocative appearance, and that made talk. But all anyone got out of *them* was that they rarely even *saw* Mr. Roulet in the house and that they obtained his supplies and house-sat and nothing else. In other words, even though some of these young ladies did indeed embrace leanings toward prostitution, no such activities had ever been requested of them from the curious Mr. Roulet.

* * * *

Jessica arrived just before noon, via taxi, at the address furnished last night. The cab fare was $62.00 but she only need pay the driver twelve due to his overzealous suggestion that she could reduce the meter by fifty dollars if she were willing to apply her mouth to a certain part of his body. About this, Jessica had no qualms.

Even before she'd checked it out, she knew she would be accepting the room and board offer from Mr. Roulet. Sight unseen or not, she couldn't stand her squalid drug-infested motel, and she was very weary of having to bend over for the manager (a back-door man) any time she was short on her rent, which was often. The police were now running stings on Backpage, and web-camming was bottoming out. She simply couldn't make ends meet. Why had her CNA accreditation not rescued her from such seedy circles? Wouldn't such a professional certificate enable to her secure respectable employment? Well, the answer is not far to seek. The only thing there were more of in Florida than old people were mosquitoes and certified nursing assistants. That fact along with a drug bust and a six-month stay, care of the county department of corrections, did little to brighten the quality of her employability.

Moving into the house of a perfect stranger she'd met online might not strike one as a sensible decision but, one, desperate situations called for desperate actions and, two, she had nothing to lose in giving it a shot. Mr. Roulet wasn't serial-killer material, was he? *Strike when the iron is hot,* her departed mother used to tell her as a child, which Jessica guessed was an axiom suggesting that one should never hesitate when presented with an opportunity. Well, the iron could scarcely get hotter than $500 a night for sitting on her ass. And if the entire gig turned out to be a sham, she'd walk out.

At any rate, here she was, at Mr. Roulet's house.

And what a house it was. *A fuckin' dump,* she observed, bags in hand as the cabbie departed. Mr. Roulet's abode was a one-story salt-box with an untrimmed yard and short palm trees half-concealing it. The new black BMW sitting there presented still more oddity. And in the blue recycle bin, atop untold scotch bottles, sat an empty 224-gram tin of Kaluga-Malossol caviar. *This is REALLY fucked up*, she thought but, strange as it might seem, she was rather at home with that. Typically, *everything* in Jessica's life was fucked up.

The drab front door presented a bizarre dull-brass knocker of a blank face: just two empty eyes, no nose, no mouth. After a shiver, she rapped on it, and the door opened, creaking in a manner that seemed appropriate of such a place and situation.

But here all that was ominous ceased, as Mr. Roulet revealed himself to be an amiable and seemingly harmless subject of study. The gray-haired and -bearded face she'd conversed with last night sat atop the body of a taller than average, obese man, past middle age. The 300-pound frame wore baggy slacks with suspenders, a huge short-sleeved white shirt, and Bruno Mali shoes. His eyes beamed, like a grandfather's upon the entry of his granddaughter. "How delightful to meet you in person, Jessica. I'm so happy you've come, and happier still that, seeing you've brought your luggage, you've decided to stay. A wise choice. Why pay rent somewhere else when you can live here for free?"

"Yes, sir," she said. "I plan to save as much money as possible so I can go back to school."

"How wonderful to encounter a young woman with goals," he said. "However, before we go on, we must take care of this one preliminary," and he proffered her a plastic cup with some powder on the bottom. Jessica knew what it was immediately.

"I'll need you to urinate in that," he told her. "Please understand that I never stereotype people but I must consider the statistical probability. Many girls who web-cam and engage in parallel professions have a proclivity towards drug addiction. I simply can't have that here, and I hope you're not offended."

Jessica chuckled and raised her jeans skirt, beneath which no panties were evident. "I'll be honest with you, Mr. Roulet. I've taken many a piss test in my time. No offense taken."

He seemed startled. "Um, well, you can do it in the bathroom, for goodness sake."

"I'd rather do it in front of you, sir. That way you'll know I'm for real. Every piss test I've taken I've had to do in front of a bull-dyke prison nurse. Lots of girls would sneak someone else's urine in in condoms. I appreciate this opportunity you're giving me, sir. I don't want you to have any doubts," and, here, she parted her legs and peed unabashed into the cup.

"Your genuineness is intriguing," he said, still taken aback. While she urinated, he did indeed watch for a moment but there was no trace of Piss-Freak in his eyes. Jessica was very familiar with this species of pervert and had urinated in front of her web-cam many a time.

Finished, she set the warm cup on the kitchen half-counter, then went around to wash her hands. "I was a drug addict a few years ago, Mr. Roulet," she admitted. "But those days are over. I've got no kids, no psycho ex-husbands or boyfriends, and no pimps. And there are no shady characters in my life. In fact, there is *no one* in my life, and I've busted my ass to make it that way."

Mr. Roulet's busy eyebrows rose. "We seem to have some commonalities, Jessica, which pleases me much. Philosopher and Noble-Prize winner Jean-Paul Sartre asserted that Hell is other people. In the course of my life I've observed that his assertion in general is oh-too-true."

Whoever this Jean-Paul guy was, she thought, *he hit that one out of the park.*

After noting the cup's negative-for-drugs result, Mr. Roulet embarked on an exposition: he'd lived in this house his entire life, and the property it sat upon had been in his family since Florida had become a U.S. territory. In fact, the current structure had been built on the original tabby-brick foundation lain in 1822. Whence did these ancestors hail? "From the northern colonies. We were Huguenots from southern France"—he paused for a muffled chuckle—"Calvinists, originally." After the Edict of Fontainebleau in 1685 essentially sanctioned the government to execute all Huguenots, the Roulets became desperate émigrés, fleeing first to the Massachusetts Bay Colony (where they were not well-received) and then to the Common Wealth of Rhode Island. "We were then kicked out of Providence in the early 1800s, for reasons...unclear," he went on. "At any rate, my forebears settled here, exactly where we are standing now." He seemed to grin. "I am the last linear male issue, so to speak, the last of a questionable yet captivating line."

Jessica noted some innuendo in his verbal thesis but she didn't care. Working for this man—however weird he really was—would give her the opportunity to turn her life back around, get back to her education and betterment, and finally sever all needs to consent to petty prostitution with disgusting slobs and never again have to debase herself before a web-cam contingent of sorry losers. She felt something now that she hadn't felt in a long time: elation.

She noticed an ornately framed map hanging on the wall: a map of the United States rendered in an older style. There seemed to be several dozen tiny red dots spread out across the states. "What's this map?" she inquired, though not with much interest. "Why all the red dots?"

"It's interesting that you'd notice," said Roulet. "The red dots, for the most part, indicate places where brutal battles took place: the French and Indian Wars, the Revolution, 1812, the Civil War, etc. Some of the dots indicate locations of, shall we say, *grim* consequence, such as," and then he pointed to a dot in Georgia, "the Andersonville Camp, where over ten thousand Union prisoners of war were left to either starve to death or die from dysentery." Next, his finger landed on Maryland, "Camp Parole, where overcrowding exhausted food supplies, therefore camp guards were ordered to cut the throats of hundreds of prisoners as they slept." Then a dot in Oklahoma, "One of the relocation points of the infamous Trail of Tears, which killed thousands of Native Americans," then another dot in California, "Truckee Lake, where seven of fifteen of the Donner Party either starved or froze to death, and were then promptly roasted and eaten. Oh, and we mustn't forget this spot here"—Roulet's finger landed on a dot marking the city of Chicago, "where a fire in 1871, strengthened by high winds, burned down quite a bit of Chicago, killing 300 and leaving 100,000 homeless. Many prisons and jails collapsed after which the more enterprising convicts formed gangs which reveled in the murder and rape of the destitute, most of whom were children."

Jessica gulped.

"Good ole America, huh?" Roulet joked. "Land of the free and home of the brave. What a disgrace. But *this,*" he clarified and pointed to a red dot in western Florida, "this dot right here, marks the location of a particularly atrocious battle between the U.S. Army and the Seminole Indians. Do you notice anything curious about that location?"

What the fuck? Jessica thought. *Why's this fruitcake have a map like this in his house?* Jessica had precious little knowledge of U.S. history but...

Something in her head seemed to click at his question. "Oh, is that where we are?"

"Why, yes it is. I commend your powers of observation. The battle I'm referring isn't found in many history books, and it took place on this very property in 1830." Roulet seemed enthused to relate this information. "I'm afraid the Indians did not fare well. Nearly a thousand were captured and then summarily executed. After the U.S. troops had run out of ammunition, they finished the slaughter with bayonets, axes, and cudgels. They kept just enough alive to bury their comrades." He chuckled. "Is it any wonder that Native Americans hate us?"

"A *thousand?*"

"Oh, yes. Plus another thousand killed in action. All buried right on this property and over several more surrounding acres."

Jessica gulped again as she considered the full force of those numbers. *Wow. America really sucks.*

"There have been occasions when I've hired landscapers to plant shrubs in the yard and their efforts have frequently dredged up bones," and then he pointed to a glass-fronted case in the corner, which displayed a variety of skulls and bones.

Gross as shit, Jessica thought.

"But enough of such cheerless reflections. Here is my room," Mr. Roulet indicated, touching the knob of the door facing the kitchen entrance. "Hopefully you will never have a need to enter it," he added with another vague, inexplicable grin.

Okaaaay...

Then he showed Jessica her own bedroom, accessed by a door at the end of the commodious—and very cluttered—living room. A small but quaint room adorned in old green wall-paper with wainscotting. An old four poster bed with a high mattress. An old dresser, an old nightstand, and an old framed engraving of some place called Mamedy, village in Europe by the looks of it. She'd never heard of the place.

"And never, for any reason, attempt to open *this* door," Mr. Roulet told her. He indicated a narrow door next to the bathroom. "It's perpetually locked, for safety purposes, an old closet in disrepair. I never use it so I've never bothered having a contractor here to fix it up."

Jessica couldn't gather how an old closet could be locked for *safety* purposes but to this notion she merely shrugged. *Fine.*

"The last time I was in it, I found quite a rats' nest. I detest all manner of vermin, as do most. I dumped poison in, and had the door permanently closed," but it was interesting how he'd said this, with a quaver in his voice, like a method actor missing his mark. *Okay by me,* she thought. *I could shit care less. All I care about is my $500 a night...*

As she turned to follow Mr. Roulet back to the living room, she noticed an *unevenness* about the carpet just before this closet door.

Warped floorboards, perhaps.

More rules of the house were expounded upon: "You must remain in the house from dusk till dawn, every night. No guests, no visitors, no relatives must ever be invited here, ever. Naturally, as a young woman I don't expect you to curtail your social life for this job, but I'm afraid that this must be pursued only between sun-up and sundown—"

"I don't have a social life, Mr. Roulet," she informed him.

"Ah, another commonality, for neither do I." He explained more: she could continue her web-camming from the house but she must never give the address to anyone. If she had "transactional clients," that was fine, but she must engage in those kinds of rendevous *removed* from the premise, and only between sun-up to sun down.

"Dusk till dawn is *my* time; I need you here; that's what you're being paid for."

"Understood, sir."

Bookshelves dominated the living room, along with a few odd portraits—the old family line, Jessica supposed. A long leather couch occupied half of the other side of the room, fronted by a glass coffee table and also a large flat-panel TV. "It's a 4k, whatever that means. Use the computer all you like, the Netflix password is taped to the table."

Goodie! she thought.

Mr. Roulet stood poised in a manner which presaged something of a coming verbal tractate. "As you've ascertained, I'm a man of eccentric habits, but I believe this offends no one when practiced without *pompier.* As an antiquary and historical scholar for my adult life's entirety, I've collected many old and unusual things—books and relics, mostly—which you now see filling this room," and his hand gestured the abundant bookshelves and their wares, and some glass display cabinets, like the bones and skulls, housing trinkets of one sort or another. "The average person might, indeed, feel certain"—he removed an old grey book from a shelf—"that a volume of mathematical tracts published by Plantin in Antwerp only 100 years after the invention of the printing press would have considerable value"—he removed an Indian arrow head from a case—"or that a Clovis point, chipped by out of calcedony by a Creek Indian 13,000 years ago must be very expensive."

"Aren't they?" Jessica asked with a knit brow. "I'd think things that old would go for big money to collectors, museums, and all that."

Roulet raised a finger, seemingly delighted. "Ah, you've alighted upon my point immediately, my dear. Here is the truth: there's precious little in this room that has any significant value. It's junk. That Plantin book? Aside from being perhaps the *dullest book ever printed*, might fetch 20 dollars at a book show. And this spear-point? One would *think* that something 13,000 years old would be worth a tidy sum but the fact is there are more of these things in America than dandelions." He put the Clovis point back. "It's all worthless to anyone but me, for sentimental reasons as they've been in my family for centuries. However—"

Jessica thought she was finally getting the message. "The stuff's worthless but the bad guys outside don't know that, and they might try to break in and steal it. Well, don't worry, Mr. Roulet. I'll guard your stuff from dusk till dawn."

"Excellent, I'm so glad you're receiving my meaning, and my explanation of my habits," the portly man went on. "Oh, and I feel I'm also obliged to let you know there are hidden cameras all over this room, but since you're a cam-girl, I can't imagine that to be a problem."

"Not a problem at all, sir—"

—"but let me hasten to add, that's only in this room and the kitchen. There are no cameras in your bedroom, nor in the bathroom."

"Wouldn't matter if there were, sir." She suspected this information was added to make her think twice about stealing anything herself. "I've been watched on cameras doing everything from taking a dump, to smearing guacamole on my butt, to stepping on jelly donuts in my bare feet."

Mr. Roulet, quite out of character, laughed aloud. "A woman of true perception. You've come to grips with the world's irrationality and *adapted* yourself to it, to your own end."

She laughed herself. "I guess you could put it that way." But one element remained that she needed some elucidation on. "Just so I'm straight on this. If someone *does* try to break into the house at night, you'll want me to call the cops, right?"

His eyebrows jumped. "No, no, you come and get me. Pound on my door till I awaken—I'm a heavy sleeper—and if I don't rouse—" He lumbered to a small framed engraving of an old manor house in moonlight, with what looked like a cloaked figure in the yard, and he took it off the wall. Taped behind it was a key. "You retrieve this at once, unlock my bedroom door, and come in and wake me up."

Cut and dry. "Got it.

"I'll need you to use your judgment. Of course, a house this old will generate its share of noises: plumbing, creaking rafters, window frames expanding, the roof settling. You'll know them when you hear them. Instead, what I'm most concerned with are *unusual* sounds, *untoward* noises, things that sound out of place or not-quite-right. Anywhere in the house, from any direction."

He must be paranoid, she assumed. *He's paying me five hundred a night to listen for noises?* Suddenly, the man's instructions were growing abstruse.

"Any odd noises from any place in the house," he went on. "This room, your bedroom, the kitchen, bathroom, laundry room, and the closet I showed you that's always locked."

Jessica nodded but, again, detected an irreducible falter, a quaver in his voice at this latest reference to the locked closet.

What is it with him and that fuckin' closet?

Yet, again, she didn't care and wouldn't question it. This whole gig was about the money and how she could better herself with it.

"I understand completely, sir, and I want you to know how grateful I am for this opportunity. But—" She paused as if to recollect herself. "What if someone tries to break in some night when you aren't here?"

"I will *always* be here, for I *never* leave the house. How's *that* for eccentric, hmm?" He smiled. "In fact, I haven't set foot out of this house in seven years."

Jessica settled into the new routine "swimmingly," and suddenly her life was pleasantly arranged in "apple-pie" order for the first time in her twenty-six years of membership with the human race. From dusk till dawn she did work at her computer while keeping an ear out for Mr. Roulet's "untoward" noises, which never revealed themselves. She would sleep early in the day, rise, and if there was a shopping list, she'd drive the car here and there to fetch the indulgences he requested, mostly exorbitantly priced Scotch and gastronomical items from gourmet stores and/or carry-out from high-end restaurants. Slabs of goose liver the size of birthday-cake slices, veal porterhouse steaks, pressed duck, oolong tea-poached Chilean sea bass, jars of truffles the size of meatballs, and the like. Once she'd brought back a steamed 12-pound lobster (12 pounds!), and once a $500 sashimi platter. And, every week, there was always the regular pickup of the aforementioned Louis XIII brandy.

During the first month of her service, she'd scarcely seen him. On rare occasions, he'd emerge from his room, take a book off the shelves, and return. Weekly, he'd leave a bag of laundry out for her to take to the cleaners. Obviously, he paid all the bills online. Thus far, all of his mail had been junk mail. She'd bring it in, leave it on the counter as directed, and while she slept, he'd come out, look it over and then transfer it into the garbage. Once a week a woman came and mowed the grass, and, odd as ever, another woman came every *day* to push a fertilizer spreader around the house. The lawn woman, named Judith, was in her early '30s, robustly figured without being fat, and had longish brunet hair turned to blond by the sun. "Oh, hi. You must be the new night-sitter." "Yes, Jessica," Jessica said. Judith was more tom-boyish than feminine, and generated something of a slutty cast: short jeans shorts and a baggy open necked t-shirt draped over massive breasts which the Florida heat immediately slicked with sweat, effecting quite a wet t-shirt show, for Judith never wore a bra. She was very much inclined for conversation, revealing that Mr. Roulet was "the best gig I've ever had, five hundred bucks a week he Paypals me, just to cut this postage stamp yard. I told him that I'd trim all the bushes and palm trees too for no extra cost but he doesn't want me too. No fertilizer, no sprinklers, nothing, that's why most of the yard is burnt. It's almost like he *wants* the place to look like shit." The same notion had occurred to Jessica more than once: a well-manicured and well-landscaped yard suggests affluence, but what burglar would be interested in a house that looked like *this?* Jessica did not have lesbian proclivities but found it impossible not to look at Judith's prodigious breasts, to which the sweat-drenched t-shirt clung like wet tissue paper. She asked, a bit impudently, "Has he ever hit on you?" "Don't I wish!" Judith laughed. "The hot weather isn't the *only* reason I wear this get-up. I'm no whore, but a guy *that* rich? I'd be spread-eagled on his floor in a blink." "He's never propositioned me," Jessica said, "but if he did...hell, a girl's gotta do what she's gotta do." "I hear that. He's got little cameras outside, everywhere. Did you know that?" "I figured as much," Jessica replied. "Told me he's got them inside too." Judith's breasts joggled once when she huffed a laugh: "If he wants eye candy, I'll give him all he wants. To keep *this* gig? Shit. It takes fifteen minutes to mow this little yard but I always take an hour, no matter how hot it is. Whenever I'm done, I take my shirt off in the backyard and hose off. I'm pretty sure he's watching. Probably beats off, hope he does."

So evidently there was a sexual side to the thus far *non*-sexual Mr. Roulet, an interesting disclosure.

Far more interesting, though, were the disclosures of Sharron, the "fertilizer girl." Sharron was healthily slim, small perky breasts, an hour-glass figure, and legs that any man would holler over. She too wore very short shorts, and always a minuscule bikini top while working, which she always removed when pushing her Scott's spreader around the fenced backyard—so, she had obviously come to the same conclusion as Judith: that Mr. Roulet was a voyeur, and Sharron had no hesitancy about emboldening her job security by practicing upon that conclusion. "But why do you only spread fertilizer around the foundation of the house?" Jessica asked. "Why not the entire yard?"

"It's not fertilizer," she said. "It's salt."

"Salt?"

"Mr. Roulet says that slugs infest the house if salt isn't put down every day. I've never seen any but so what? I'm not about to tell him there are far better ways to keep slugs off. For $500 a day, seven days a week? I'll do cartwheels in the yard dressed like Batman while whistling Dixie if he wants."

So it seemed that Sharron made more money for less time than anyone—a dream job, and for something he could get neighborhood kids to do for ten bucks.

"Have you met the maids yet?"

"Maids? No," Jessica said, "but I sleep during the day so they may have come then."

"Once a week three chicks from MAIDS R US come here and clean the kitchen, bathroom, and living room. All buck naked."

"Wow."

So much for *speculation* about voyeurism.

"But he doesn't even watch them," Sharron went on. "Stays in his room the whole time."

"Probably watches on cameras. He must be bashful."

"Whatever. All I know is he saved my ass. I was practically homeless, living with scumbags and dope-slingers; my life was a pile of shit. But now? I got a nice new car, a great place to live, and a bunch of cash in the bank. Honestly, if that man pulled his cock out in front of me, I'd ask no questions, I'd just get on my knees and suck."

"Me, too," Jessica knew. "Business is business." Perhaps this was a universal perspective, today and for all of human history. The Powers That Be in this world considered average people to be "the little people," and it was hard to make ends meet, doubly so for women. The contingent of society that label such activities as immoral were the "haves," not the "have nots." Every night Jessica did *not* have to sleep under a bridge was proof of initiative and resolve.

The last datum Sharron revealed was the manner by which she first came in contact with Mr. Roulet: web-camming.

Smooth sailing ensued for the first month of Jessica's employ. She sat up nights, spent time on the internet investigating various online courses she might want to take and school applications. She bid a hearty good-riddance to her web-cam account. She watched movies, and she started a mild regimen of exercise: sit-ups, push-ups, etc. She often spent her entire shift nude or just in panties. In the event that Mr. Roulet *was* observing her, she wanted to make damn sure he was satisfied with what he saw. Several times a week, she'd masturbate on the couch in the middle of the night, and would bring herself to genuine orgasm, not the kind she'd faked so often on the web-cam.

Not that she was of an inquisitive turn, every now and then, Jessica she might take note of some decorative aspect of the big living room. For instance, a framed photo—smaller than the old map of red dots—which showed a vast background of old buildings somewhere, fronted by cobblestone streets. The buildings were gayly painted, but the foreground showed several berms that had brick walls built into them, under great mounds of earth. Jessica squinted at a bottom corner and made out: *Kaunas' Seventh Fort Barracks, Lithuania.* Jessica smirked. *Okay, what's the big deal with this place?*

So she Goggled it on her phone.

"What the FUCK?" she said out loud. An internet site revealed that the Kaunas Seventh Fort was a military garrison and weapons depot in World War 1 and later, during World War II, the Nazis had converted it into a death camp. Over 50,000 civilians had been executed there; often the victims were cremated alive, to increase efficiency and conserve ammunition.

Jessica was revolted firstly and, secondly, dumbfounded. Between this and the larger map which showed battle-sites and locations of considerable atrocities, Jessica could not reckon at all why Mr. Roulet would choose such macabre wall hangings as decor. *To each his own, I guess,* came the thought, and then she wandered down the wall to inspect one of the old bookshelves. This wasn't much of a conscious effort but suddenly here eyes began to take stock of the titles on the shelves: *The Necrophiles* by David Gurney, *The Perversities of the Marquis de Sade: A Clinical Analysis* by Anthony Cadman, *A History of Trepanation.* Jessica blinked. She had no idea what trepanation meant so she Goggled it and blanched. Evidently it was the process of cutting a hole in someone's skull for the purpose of torture or to release evil spirits. *Are you fuckin' shitting me!* Jessica thought. The next book read *Satanic Sexual Ritual* and the next *The Compendium of Crime Scene Photographs.* Jessica's hands shook as she slid out this latter tome, which more resembled a coffee-table picture book. Flipping just through a few pages knotted her stomach and almost made her vomit. The photographer seemed to have a penchant for photos of female victims of sexually related homicides.

Jessica winced and put the book back, appalled. Roulet was clearly a first-rate pervert and sicko. *Books like that shit must turn him on, those photos get his dick hard,* she realized. A library that seemed to highlight all manner of sexual aberration? And a map of the worst atrocities in American history?

That night she tried to watch TV but there seemed to be only horror movies available. *No thanks...* She ordered herself to think more precisely about Mr. Roulet and her job here. *People into shit like that HAVE to be royally fucked up in the head.* And this reasonable consideration urged her to question herself. Was she actually endangering herself by being here? Was the risk worth the rewards? *Maybe I should quit,* she thought. *It's a good bet that any guy with books like THAT is a genuine psych-job. He could even be a killer...*

Yes, maybe she should just quit.

But the more she thought about it, the more unlikely it seemed. The truth was, Mr. Roulet was a fat, out-of-shape old man. *I'm young and strong, he's old and fat. Even I could kick his ass.*

Therefore, the path of least resistance won out. The money was too good, and in spite of the man's taste in reading material, there was nothing threatening about him. If anybody knew a psycho when she saw one, it was Jessica.

And Roulet wasn't it. Maybe he was a bit stuffy but he was a nice guy and a fat putz. *He's harmless,* she decided. *This job is dynamite. Why let some other girl rake in MY money? Fuck that.*

So it was settled. She was overreacting to a bunch of books on Roulet's shelf.

Next, she perused a second shelf, whose books were more obscure. *A Comprehensive Study of the Voynich Manuscript,* was one title, which she could make neither heads nor tails of. Inside was peppered with color plates of what looked like children's coloring. *Big deal,* Jessica thought. Next, *The Clavicule of Solomon,* which contained an introduction in English but the rest of the book was in some foreign language Jessica couldn't guess at. *Hebraic Symbology,* was the next; it was full of geometric drawings and odd symbols. *What a bunch of boring shit,* she thought, but at least it was tamer than the first books she'd happened upon. She was about to call it quits when a more intricately bound book caught her eye. She pulled it out.

Deadpasses & Ethereal Egression read the gold-leaf title. This one seemed newer than the other books. When she opened it randomly, she found that several pages in the center were shiny photoplates of maps. One map depicted an area in Israel under which was the legend PHANTASMAL CONDUITS OF MARJ IBN AMIR (MEGIDDO). *I got no idea what the FUCK that is,* Jessica realized, *and I got no idea why the FUCK I'm looking at this stupid book...* However, the next plate caused some flash of recognition: it was a geographical map of the United States and Canada, this one was sprinkled with tiny red dots just like the older map on the wall. The legend read: KNOWN & PROBABLE ACTIVE DEADPASSES IN NORTH AMERICA. Jessica walked the book to the wall map, and leaned over, squinting.

Quite a few of the locations in the book coincided with those on the map. Andersonville, Georgia. Chicago, Illinois. Truckee Lake, California.

Jessica just shook her head and put the book away, then decided to forget about the entire bizarre business.

In that first month, Jessica had seen Mr. Roulet exactly three times, for less than five minutes per appearance, and in those minutes, he'd proved himself to be—just as Jessica had suspected—no more than a harmless fat putz. And in that same month, she had experienced absolutely nothing that might be considered "untoward." No odd noises, no disturbances of any kind, and no evidence of prowlers.

It was a Thursday morning, an hour after sun-rise, when Jessica concluded her shift, ate a bowl of cereal, watched ten minutes of local news, then went outside and put the garbage and recycle bin out by the curb. She spared a chuckle at the copious number of expensive Scotch bottles in the bin, then she spared a moment to notice the swath of salt that ran along the foundations of the house, shaking her head. She went back into the house.

No errands awaited her on the list; so she could either relax, go for a drive, whatever. She decided to go to the beach for a little while, before going to bed at noon. This had all the makings of a nice, quiet, laid-back day.

After a quick shower, the stature of the day changed.

When she alighted from the bathroom, drying her hair, her heart surged. Mr. Roulet was lying on the floor, half out of his room. His bulky shape was shivering.

Fuck! She acted instantly, lunging, flipping him over, feeling for pulse. *Heart attack,* she could only presume. She blew one short breath into his mouth, then straddled him to apply heart compressions. He lolled back and forth; it was as if she were straddling a manatee. Just as she thought, *Shit shit shit! This big fucker's gonna die!* he seemed to stabilize a little. "You're gonna be okay, Mr. Roulet," she blabbered. "I'm calling 911—"

"No!" he gasped.

She called, then pulled on a robe. "No if's, and's, or but's." She got back down on a knee to make feeble attempts to comfort him. "They'll be here soon, they'll get you fixed up," all the while thinking, *If you didn't stuff your face with caviar and lobster and drink like Charlie Fuckin' Sheen, you wouldn't be in this mess!*

He pointed to his open bedroom door, gasping. "Amethyst. On chain. And leather pouch. On my dresser..."

What the fuck? He was probably terrified and insensible due to the attack's reduction of oxygen to the brain. *Hallucinotic,* she recalled from dim CNA classes. She went hesitantly into a bedroom—a huge, dark, commodious chamber—composed mostly of shadows which half-concealed bookshelves, old portraits, knickknacks, etc. She found the dark-clotted dresser. *Amethyst, did he say? What the fuck? And a pouch...*

There they were, the crudely cut semi-precious gem on a silver chain, and a small leather touch with drawstring. She inserted her finger in the latter, felt powder, and immediately considered heroin or cocaine. But it was more granulated and when she tasted a few granules on her fingertip she realized:

Salt.

She paused a moment before rushing back to her felled employer. She noticed several small unmistakable objects also on the dresser: at least four 128-gig SD cards.

Sirens blared outside. She darted back to the foyer, opened

the front door, then returned to one knee beside Mr. Roulet. A crabbed hand snatched the amethyst and pouch, and he gasped "Thank you, Jessica..."

She grabbed his other hand. "Here are the EMT guys, don't worry, Mr. Roulet, you'll be fine in a jiffy," and very swiftly two young medical attendants were in the house, lifting their obese charge onto a collapsible gurney with surprising ease, and were wheeling him out into daylight that had not touched his face in seven years. Jessica trotted after him. "I'll lock up the house and follow you to the hospital, Mr. Roulet—"

"No!" he wheezed. "Stay here! I'll call if, if—"

"There's no 'if's, Mr. Roulet. You'll be fine. I'll see you real soon..."

The gurney snapped into the back of the ambulance, the doors slammed shut. Jessica stood ineptly in the middle of the street, watching wide-eyed as ambulance sped away.

Of all the fucked up things, she thought. *There goes my cash cow. What am I gonna do if he dies?*

Her most immediate notion was to go to the hospital right now and check his status. The modest medical data she'd gleaned from her old CNA classes made her think that he would probably survive. He'd been conscious when the EMTs took him, and he hadn't looked like one at the foot of death's door. But in the event of his death, Jessica knew she'd be sling-shotted right back to web-camming and all the seediness that companioned it. *Damn it,* she thought. *Don't croak, buddy. PLEASE don't croak...*

She snapped up the keys, was just about to go to the car, but stopped where she stood. For whatever reason, Roulet didn't want her leaving the house, so....

I better say put. Calling the hospital for a status report, she knew, would be useless; these days no medical information about anyone would be relayed via the phone unless Mr. Roulet granted such access.

Idly, then, she moseyed around the living room, as she had may times, amid all its old books and relics. She knew that Mr.

Roulet's assertion that these possessions were all worthless was mere posturing. Rich men owned expensive things and some of this would certainly be valuable. However, Jessica knew she wasn't crummy enough a person to steal. And as for the grotesque books of crime-scene photos, and about genocides and tragedies, who would want to buy them?

Then another speculation occurred to her...

If Mr. Roulet died...well, would it still be stealing then? He'd already told her there were no heirs. *And God knows what kind of valuables he's got in his room...*

His room.

The door to his bedroom remained opened from the mishap. Dare she enter for an expedient look around? What harm could there be? And Mr. Roulet could hardly object...

No second thoughts followed her back into the dark chamber. The opened door provided nearly all illumination but as her vision acclimated, the graininess began to divulge details: tall shelves, glass cases, undecipherable framed pictures. An immense antique bed. Imprints of other doors formed, no doubt to the bathroom and a private kitchen. A bank of wide computer monitors behind a desk filled one corner, presumably Mr. Roulet's work station and surveillance post for all of his supposed hidden cameras, but the monitors were all off. She pulled open some desk drawers and found stack of photos, each showing Roulet at a variety of ages. One showed Roulet with a hat on, and in the background stood a some kind of tan fortress in bright sun; on the back, in handwriting, were the words *Ziggurat of Ur, Iraq, 1999.* Next, a decrepit ruin of old blocks and crumbling foundations, and a ancient of some kind in the far distance, Roulet stood in the foreground, sharing his eyes. *Capernaum deadpass, April, 1988,* read the writing on the back. Another: Roulet, a bit older, staring into a camera before a scrubby field centered by a huge igloo-like erection of bricks and very u-shaped ports in its walls. *Maxon, Georgia, 2011*, this one was inscribed. *DP at the Gast Furnace.* Jessica shook her head. She recalled the word *deadpass* from one of Roulet's books but she couldn't guess what it meant. *These must be photos of places Roulet traveled to during his life,* she figured. But next...

An 11"x14" framed picture sat on the dresser, and she picked it up to turn it toward the light.

A wave of nausea accosted her; she winced, gagged, and put the picture back. *Fuck me...*

It was a demented oil painting apparently, reminding her of the famous old paintings and engravings by Hieronymus Bosch and Gustav Dore: graphic illustrations of Hell. What Jessica had absorbed in that single glimpse looked like a bacchanal of netherworldly lust, a triptych panel suggesting the everlasting sins of the flesh in some deep recess of perdition. The vision shifted like vertigo in her head: a meld of concepts. Was it a cave, a cavern of some kind, lit by torches? But what the cave wall surrounded could only be described as something like a grandstand or bleachers—rows of seats for *spectators.* Jessica couldn't fathom this. *What a fucked up idea for a painting...* Most fucked up, however, were the activities of the figures populating this appalling artwork. Gaunt and grinning demons converged among the nude throng, arms buried to the elbows in vaginas, rectums, and cranked open mouths. Other bulkish craggy-looking creatures yanked off heads, arms, legs, breasts without discrimination, using taloned, dinner-plate-sized hands the color of slug-skin. Horns rose from their slab-like heads, their mouths jammed with fangs like shards of plate glass. But the inhuman were not the only participants: two men who were rotten but very much alive effected a double-penetration upon a woefully young woman; Jessica only hoped that it was a mistake of the artist that he'd depicted the victim as more adolescent than adult. Another female, just as young, had been fettered to a wooden table, legs spread so wide her hips must've been broken. Her face froze like the visage in Munch's "The Scream."

She was outrageously pregnant, and at her belly's highest elevation there was the point of a manual brace-drill about to be cranked by a cloaked and hooded figure.

But strangest of all was this bizarre "grandstand" in the scene. Fancily attired men and women sat there watching either raptly or casually. Most smiled in amusement at the fete taking place at the center of the establishment...

Jessica gagged again at the recollection, going light-headed, then stumbled around in the bedroom's dark crannies feeling for some evidence of Mr. Roulet's fancy Scotch. Eventually, her hand fell on a bottle and she staggered back out to the kitchen.

"Holy fuck, holy fuck, holy fuck!"

She took a long chug off the bottle, her eyes widened, then she swallowed. The refined liquid burned down her throat and bloomed in her belly. *How do people drink that shit?* she thought, outraged, but a moment later the much-needed buzz kicked in.

Fuck. Who would paint such a perverted picture? What kind of warped artist would even think of such a concept for a piece of artwork? And worse... *Only a really warped person would want something like that...*

Mr. Roulet. If the books on his shelves weren't enough, that painting was.

And there was something else, wasn't there?

She went back into the darkened bedroom, her motives on auto-pilot. It wasn't to look at the picture again—God, no—it was for the SD cards she'd seen.

The work of a moment had the cards in her hand and herself seated at the big computer screen before the couch. She snapped the first card into the slot, and opened the file, and was never the same again...

She sped to the hospital in an enraged daze. She no longer had a speck of concern for Roulet's well-being, she only wanted to confront him. She couldn't vomit anymore because there was nothing left to throw up. She'd collected all the SD cards, jammed them in her pocket, and headed to the hosptial. Her plan was to confront Roulet with the cards and demand an explanation.

It was as simple as this: that painting of the spectators in Hell and all its atrocious trimmings was devised from reality, a rendition of an image in a photograph, and the photograph had been a frame off one of the 4-hour SD cards she'd found on Roulet's dresser.

She hadn't been able to watch the entire thing; she doubted

if any sane person could. The place in the painting was real: the spectator pit or whatever it was, situated in some forsaken, Hadean grotto lit by torches of burning pitch. All the carnal and charnel horror of the painting unfolded before Jessica's eyes in High Def 1080p. The camera roved leisurely about as though it were the eye of casual onlooker. One atrocity after another, for hours, unrolled on the screen, all that she'd seen in the noxious painting and a hundred times more. Several spectators sitting aside to watch seemed to *nod* to the camera as if the bearer were an acquaintance. Among such spectators were a finely dressed elderly couple, tonsured men in sackcloth surplices, a woman with skin as black as volcanic glass, her bald head beaded with intricate scars, her earlobes hooped and her neck extended half a foot past the norm via brass bands. One young modern couple kissed lewdly and fondled each other's crotch; they wore matching shirts that read LUSTMORD next to whom stood a man in the regalia of a Roman legionnaire, circa 100 B.C. All stared intently at the horrific atrocities taking place, some masturbating with nonchalance.

Nauseous, Jessica removed the card and inserted another. This one depicted a different location, the camera venturing deeper through a stone-arched corridor tinged white by nitrous encrustations. Fewer torches burned here, perhaps a good thing, for every few yards a recess appeared, each revealing more atrocities and cacodemoniacal sex acts which trebled the tenor of those in the pit of spectators. The camera never lingered long over each revelation, moving in and out, in and out. The attendants here were clearly not human, for humans didn't have great wings folded behind them, nor prick ears, nor horned heads. They seemed to be supervising the goings-on of more of those slab-like things she recalled most distinctly from the painting, those tartarean ushers with chisel-slits for eyes, flesh like slug-skin stretched tight over massive musculatures, mouths like knife-slits in clay. In each chamber, these things were either raping women to living-death, bare-handedly dismembering humans and unhumans alike; eviscerating, castrating, and exsanguinating others in place; and filling occupied bathtub-sized vessels with red-hot coals—

all this while grinning in demonian glee. At that point, Jessica had ejected this second SD card and put her face in her hands, shuddering.

The rest tried to recollect itself in her head but she forced it aside, parked in the visitors lot, and walked hurriedly into the hospital, unabashed by her parsimonious apparel (flipflops, short cut-offs, and a yellow tube top) and not caring in the least that stock was being taken of her. The SD cards in her shorts pocket seemed to vibrate with heat; just knowing they were there made her nauseous again. "I'm here to visit a patient named Edmund Roulet," she droned to an elderly woman at the info desk. "What room is he in?"

"Edmund Roulet, you say?" The woman seemed hesitant, off track. "Yes, uh, please have a seat. Someone will be with you shortly," and then she picked up the phone in a manner that seemed furtive.

Jessica sat down in the empty waiting lounge, still nerve-racked. *Why not just tell me what room to go to? Unless...*

The inclination dawned on her now that Mr. Roulet must've died, and soon a doctor or nurse would come down to notify her. *FUCK, I hope that fat sicko didn't croak. I've GOT to find out what's on these cards...,* and it was then that the last bit of footage she'd watched drifted back into her head: the unseen cameraman wandering about in the rear coves of that diabolical undercroft. She'd already guessed that the "cameraman" could only be Roulet himself, and this was verified in the next few frames when the image crossed an oval-shaped mirror in whose silver veins could be seen the face and chest of a younger, slimmer Mr. Roulet, with a tiny lapel camera concealed on his shirt pocket.

One more chamber would be examined before Jessica, clenching in nausea, would turn the screen off.

Like a floating eye, the camera drifted into the next appalling, stone compartment. Women, clearly, were the victims of choice in these chasms, and the woman in question now had been lain out on a stone slab (nude, of course, and semen-covered), shackled down, and convulsing as the slug-fleshed denizens applied some sort of bucket-like apparatus over her head. Etched pictographs, geometric glyphs, and words in an unknown language covered the helmet-like device.

Obviously, some occult science was taking place as others gathered round to spectate, including one of the horned, perfectly bosomed she-demons whose shining flawless skin seemed to shift in and out of various dark pearlescent colors. She clasped her long-nailed fingers as she watched the ensuing horrors. Next to her stood what appeared to be one of the rotten male cadavers Jessica has glimpsed on the first card.

The woman on the slab bucked insanely; smoke poured from around the opening of the helm-like device, and muffled screams could be heard—screams of such tenor and hideousness that they could never be accurately described. A moment of tense anticipation rose in the room until finally the smoke subsided and the screams degraded into sluggish blurbering.

When one of the monstrous acolytes removed the "bucket," it could be seen that the entirety of the woman's head had been collapsed; hair, nose, ears, and mouth still intact, but as if her skull had been removed, leaving a slack, quivering sack of flesh with eyelids that opened and closed over nothing.

What had become of her skull?

The skull, still complete with roving, lidless eyeballs, was removed from the "bucket" and then placed on a wall of shelving alongside dozens of other such flesh-denuded heads. Now a spectator, an ordinary human man, climbed onto the slab to commence fornicating with the quivering, skull-less victim. It was at this time-stamp that Jessica snapped the SD card out of the slot, and tripped away to vomit.

"Miss?"

Jessica's fugue-state of memory dissipated like fog, and through it she saw a tall, broad-shouldered man with short, greyed hair, dressed in a well-tailored suit. It was not the doctor or nurse she expected, but a police detective with his badge clipped to his jacket pocket.

"I'm Lieutenant Spence of the Metro PD Homicide Section."

"Homicide?" she muttered. "So he's—"

"I regret to inform you that Edmund Roulet is dead. Cause of death is as yet undetermined; however, it's clear that it was murder via some mode of extreme and unrepresentative violence."

This was far more than she expected. She stared up at the immense, well-dressed man.

"If you'll follow me, please," he said.

Up the elevator they went, with Jessica droningly answering his salvo of questions. "No, not a friend, really, I was his house-sitter and I ran errands for him." "No, I don't think he had any direct acquaintances, and no family." "No, in fact, he *never* left the house. He told me he hasn't for seven years." "I'm an ex cam-girl and, yeah, I know what you're thinking but, no, nothing romantic, intimate or sexual ever happened between us." "My overall impression? He was a recluse interested in anthropology and mythology and stuff like that." "No, nobody ever visited him at the house. I almost never saw him."

More cursory inquiries followed as Spence nodded to a uniformed cop posted in front of a patient room. Before Spence opened the door, he said, "I need you to identify the body. I need to know that he is the same man on his license."

"I don't get it," Jessica said. "Isn't his face the same as the face on his ID?"

Spence looked at her deadpan. Then he led her into the room.

Jessica looked at the man in the bed beside the plaque which read ROULET, EDMUND, screamed, "You gotta be shitting me!" and ran back out of the room.

Still deadpan, Spence walked out to where she leaned gasping against the wall. "Fuck!" she bellowed.

Spence's brow rose. "That's him, I take it?"

"Yes..."

"How can you be sure?"

"The chain around his neck, the amethyst, and the leather pouch in his hand. It's salt."

"Salt, amethyst?"

"He asked for them when the ambulance was coming."

"Why?"

"I don't know. He asked for them so I got them."

"Hmm." Spence pinched his chin. "His fingerprints aren't on file, but we're checking with his banks. Dental records, of course, will be useless."

"Forget all that shit. It's him," she said, staring at the wall opposite.

"Over the course of my career, I've seen a fair share of bizarre things. But I've never seen anything even close to *this*."

Yeah, but I have, Jessica thought, because atop the body in the room there was no head where a head should be, just a skull-less sack of flesh, bearded, slack-mouthed, slits for eyes behind which no eyeballs existed.

"And you say he asked you for *salt* and *amethyst?*"

"Yes."

"Do you know why?"

Some kind of protection, I guess. But why say that? "No, I don't."

Spence went on, "There are security cameras all over this hospital but my people checked them all. No one ever entered that room except for a few doctors and shift nurses. I don't know how that's possible." He squinted at her. "Did he have any enemies that you know of?"

"It sure looks like it," Jessica whispered, "but not that I know of."

Jessica stayed in a motel for the three days the police were examining the house. When she returned, she cleared the infamous yellow police tape off the front door, and found the inside in fair order, though much had been taken: all of Roulet's computers, a good many books from the shelves, even her own laptop, which she was told would be returned "when the investigation was complete." Dustings of purple fingerprint powder were evident. Though she only ventured a little way into Roulet's darkened room, it was clear the chamber had been turned upside down. Several of the murky pictures on the wall were gone, confiscated, and so was the appalling painting on the dresser.

Oddest of all was that narrow door next to the bathroom, the door sealed, Roulet had claimed, because of a past rat infestation. Police had taken the door down (and made no neat job of it) but no closet existed behind it, just house-frame and very old plywood. No evidence of a former rodent problem could be seen, no old cakes of poison, etc. It was a door to nowhere, and its location made no sense. The uneven carpet just before it had been pulled up, the cause of the unevenness easily viewed. Not warped floorboards (the bare floor was concrete) but instead an inch-thick layer of salt.

More salt. He'd had salt spread around the house every day, and even took a pouch of it to the hospital with him. A quick Google search on her phone verified her earlier idea: that salt was thought to possess protective properties such as absorbing negative psychic energy and warding off malevolent spirits. Ancient magic circles were made of salt. No unholy being could enter a salt-circle. *He blocked that door with it, and kept a circle of it around his house,* she reasoned. *And the thing he feared the most never got him here. It came to the hospital instead...and got him there...*

Oh, well...

She supposed she would be able to stay in the house until the power was shut off, or some legal authority sealed it for probate, but the month-plus of salary she'd earned thus far was all in the bank and would cover rent somewhere else for a long time.

Things could be worse, she thought.

But not for Roulet.

She knew it was some inner-monitor which goaded her to stay for awhile: the inclination that there was something she should wait for, which proved correct several nights later, a stormy, rainy night, of all things, and at midnight.

She came awake in the old four-poster bed to a rustling sound from beyond her room. She felt no inkling of fear when she rose and walked out, wearing only panties. The matter-of-fact thought entered her head, *They've arrived.*

The front door stood open. When Jessica took a step out of her bedroom and looked around, she very quickly saw the impossible...

A bald, nude woman with inscrutable, shifting skin stood smiling in the middle of the living room. Over six feet tall, with heavy orbicular breasts and a hairless cleft pubis. Black horns jutted from her head, and when she grinned more broadly, doglike fangs showed in her mouth.

Jessica had seen her before.

But another figure was also in the room, a darkened figure who seemed to be surveying one of the bookshelves. It was a man, a dead man, a *rotten* man, the likes of whom she'd seen previously on the SD cards.

"Please excuse this intrusion, miss," he said in a fluttery voice. "I'll be brief. How this rendevous concludes is entirely up to you."

"You," she said. "You're from that place."

"Indeed, we are, and we're here to reclaim what is ours."

"So. The salt around the house doesn't work?"

"Well enough, except when it rains." He smiled sharp as a knife. "Edmund Roulet was steadfast with his locks and guards, but they only suffice here. We knew it was only a matter of time before some necessity forced him to leave his abode. And this place, I'll add, is something of a sacred property, one of many ancient, disused ingresses. The land this house sits on is one of them. It's called a Deadpass. To us, time is rather insignificant; however, that portal"— he aimed a decompased finger at the torn down closet door—"has existed for a long time. Roulet knew all about it. He was, you might say, an hereditary member, the last of a long line of valued patrons. But he violated the rules, and that is unpardonable. He took from us, so we took from him."

"He deserved to be *murdered?*" she questioned.

"Oh, but he hasn't been murdered at all. In fact, Roulet is very much alive and always will be," and then the man snapped his dead fingers, and the bald woman—with luminous skin merging between lavender and molten orange—produced one of the "helmet"-like objects, a thing like a bucket crawling with glyphs. From inside, she withdrew a wet, skinned skull, complete with lidless eyeballs.

"Brother Roulet will be with us always, in a very special place," said the living corpse. "You see, there are many Deadpasses throughout this awful world, the thresholds of which will allow the admittance only of those with certain hereditary and long-standing privileges—those from bloodlines that have, shall we say, served our benefactor proudly. Roulet was sired by such a line and was once highly regarded and trusted. But over time, as is sometimes the case, his greed and his pride violated our very specific and exclusive bylaws which must be obeyed to the letter. Our lairs, or Deadpasses, are time-held preternatural secrets but Roulet had the gall—"

"To photograph them," Jessica realized. "He videotaped them."

The dead man nodded. "Such an act can *never* be tolerated." Then he turned more solemn, almost forlorn. "You are an innocent, and it's my deepest wish that we need not use our device on you, in which case you would be joining your former employer forever."

"I think I know what you want," Jessica blurted. She ran back to her bedroom, withdrew the SD cards from her shorts, then returned.

She dropped the cards into the living cadaver's opened hand.

His eyes deeply searched hers. "How rare and wonderful, to encounter someone genuinely honest." His hand closed over the cards. "Thank you. We'll intrude upon you no more."

Jessica looked behind her, at a sound. The horned woman—which Jessica could only presume was some sort of succubus or demon—was wielding an ordinary broom and sweeping a path through the salt before the opening where the closet door had been taken down.

"Thank you, Jessica," fluttered the voice of the corpse. "Should the end of your life bring you to us, rest assured, you will be shown favor," and then the corpse and his companion stepped into the oblong opening and melted away until all that remained were the old two-by-fours of the wall-frame and plywood.

Jessica remained where she stood, eye-eyed, her skin tingling and her nerves frayed. *I think*, she reckoned, *that I'm gonna start going to church real soon.*

AFTERWORD

I feel it necessary to offer a few words regarding the provenance of this piece. A number of years ago I was solicited, along with a good many fine writers, to write a short story set in the creative domain of another author. That author is my friend and outstanding writer Gerard Houarner. That creative domain, of course, is Gerard's infamous Painfreak, one of the most thrilling and unique creations in the annals of Extreme Horror fiction. I don't remember what year, but some time back, Necro Publications endeavored to produce a horror anthology in which each story deals with Gerard's wonderful (and appalling!) creation, and included in it was a longish piece that I wrote, entitled "The Night-Sitter." It wouldn't have been right for me to reprint that story verbatim here simply because its impetus directly involves Gerard's creative property. But it is a fun story so I retooled it, removed the components that involved Painfreak, and replaced them with something generic. I hope you enjoy my little rewrite. And, moreover, I thank Gerard in the first place for allowing me the honor of playing in his "sandbox." It was a lot of fun!
E.L.

AN AMERICAN
TOURIST
IN POLAND

Among the cities of significance in the great country of Poland, Wroclaw holds an esteemed standing. It boasts a Catholic Archdiocese, over seventy churches, a brick wall dating back to the 1100s, and many McDonald's hamburger places which are distinguished by being exponentially better than any McDonald's in America.

As for famous locals, there is no shortage: Alois Alzheimer, Baron Manfred von Richthofen, Peter Lorre, and Louis M. Cohn, the chief suspect as the starter of the Great Chicago Fire in 1871 which killed 300 people and left 100,000 homeless.

Wroclaw, it needs to be mentioned, is not pronounced "Row-claw" as one might expect but instead "Vrush-lahv" or "Vrots-swav," or something like that. In other words, the language makes little sense to English ears and eyes. For instance, the most popular beer in Wroclaw—and perhaps in the entire country—is spelled Zywiec. You might suspect this would be pronounced as "Zee-wick," but, no, it's pronounced "Shiv-itch." This fact is likely accounted for by the Polish language, which possesses not 26 but 32 letters, and nine vowels, not five, plus multitudinous accents; and there are other mind-bending or phonological reasons.

But, enough of the language. Wroclaw rests on the 500-mile long River Oder, known for its great beauty and its propensity for flash floods. The city had been almost entirely destroyed by the Russians in World War Two, because Wroclaw, then known as Breslau, was part of Germany's Third Reich. On an incidental note, the city was the very last stronghold to surrender to the Allies, one day before the Reich's unconditional surrender. Hitler himself thought highly of the city, visiting often, and was known to take long, solitary walks about the massive Centennial Hall, built by the famous architect Max Burg as a commemoration of Napoleon's final defeat at the Battle of Leipzig, which ended at last the French scourge of Europe. More than that, Hitler's ghost is said to be seen regularly walking about the Hall's fountain and gardens.

Ah, but this is not a tourist brochure...

There are excellent hotels in Wroclaw. The Mercure and the Orbis could not be more pleasing, nor can their rates—to Americans anyway—be scoffed at. To the U.S. wallet, in fact, Wroclaw's prices are at least one-third cheaper—for everything. Everything, that is, save for gasoline and real estate. But these latter factors do not concern the average American tourist, and it is one such tourist of whose experiences I have to tell you now.

This gentleman, named Foster Morley—from Florida—had visited Wroclaw once, and he declared to me that it was the most beautiful city he has ever traveled to, and brimming with the most beautiful people.

However, after his second trip, in spite of all his accolades, he has not returned, nor will he ever. Perhaps this narrative will shed light on the reason why.

Morley alighted quite happily, bags in hand, from the front doors of the overly tidy Wroclaw Airport, smiling as brightly as the afternoon sun. In fact, during his previous visit, he'd never experienced an iota of bad weather.

Commercially, the airport was known as *Copernicus* Airport, named for the famous mathematician/astronomer who first identified the fact that the sun, not the earth, was the center of our solar system (which wasn't actually true because the Greek astronomer Aristarchus of Samos, nearly 2000 years previous, stated that fact in writing, but still…) Nicholaus Copernicus was a first order genius and scholar, and one of the smartest men to be walking the earth during his lifetime (1473-1543, for those interested.) Genius, yes, but perhaps a matter of the author's indulgence forces him to cite the rather flawed Danish astronomer, Tycho Brahe, who believed that the sun orbited the earth, and who lost his nose in a sword fight against a cousin after a drunken squabble over a woman at someone's wedding. But as a nobleman, Brahe was quickly fitted with a false nose made of brass, silver, gold, or bronze—no one knows for sure. Brahe died in 1601 when his bladder ruptured during a banquet in Prague. Ah, and what has this to do with our American protagonist Mr. Foster Morley? Nothing whatsoever, but I include it here because I find it interesting.

Upon Mr. Morley's full entitlements we need not dwell. It should suffice to say that he was a man past middle age (50-odd) and a gentleman of leisure—in that he needed no actual employment, having, it seemed, enough money of his own to fund his life. He'd taken a fine degree at Dartmouth but did little with it besides pursue his own delvings into scholarship for his own satisfaction. One might describe him as a tallish, palish, baldish, stoutish, gray-bearded man, and though not at all unpleasant in demeanor, he proved to be not much of a social creature, not a "People Person," as I believe the saying goes. He was very much alone in the world, and lived very much *by* himself and *to* himself, and felt quite content in this domestic state of solitude. It need not be mentioned, then, that neither chick nor child (as the British say) adorned his existence, and if they ever did, well, that would've been thought of by neighbors as the injection of a very new and *incongruous* element into what they knew of the life of Mr. Foster Morley.

His closest confidantes existed as a small cadre of online correspondents (I myself being one such member) who enjoyed sharing communiques which detailed mutual interests—mainly scholarly enlightenment and descriptions of travels in other countries. A stodgy troupe, in other words, with leanings toward the arrogant, the pedantic, and intellectual one-ups-manship. For some reason, though, I seemed to enjoy a slightly more confidential friendship with Mr. Morley, for I, and I only, knew something the others didn't. Though a man of the keenest antiquarian and architectural pursuits, Morley was also—to use his own words—an "emissary of poly-national libidiny." Now, you may be wondering just what that convoluted term means—just as I wondered. Hence, the reason for my setting this down at such length.

Taxis in Poland all seem to be operated by leather-jacketed, well-groomed men who are not prone to idle chatter, and they all seem to drive shiny Mercedes sedans. It was into the backseat of one such sedan that Morley installed his bodily bulk while the driver stowed the baggage. Momentarily, the meter was engaged and the car smoothly departed along the airport's exit loop. A rearward glance rewarded Morley with a stunning view of the facility, which seemed derived from a Bauhausian architectural blueprint: beauty through functionality, and this impression was only exemplified by the day's current weather: sunny, mild, and scarcely a cloud in the sky, a real pearl of a day.

Morley had already informed the driver of his general destination. "Centrum," he'd said, "but give me a minute to find the hotel address." Centrum was the universal designation for the City Center, one of the most delightful places Morley had ever seen on earth. Further description will be detailed when the proper time comes, but for the overall look of Wroclaw, a few words must be supplied. Never in his life had Morley seen such a drastic clash of architecture, but here the word "clash" mustn't be interpreted as a quality of discord. First, for instance, as they exited the airport, long, low rows of Communist Bloc-era buildings greeted the eye; military barracks, apparently, but long out of use. Barbed wire fences surrounded them, while the faded, gray cement walls were divoted by innumerable bullet strikes which—Morley had heard—were the result of Polish troops celebrating the end of the former Soviet Union's stranglehold on the country. *Perhaps they let it remain standing as a reminder that times were not always so good,* Morley reflected. Yet when the Mercedes turned through a roundabout, the first thing he noticed was a bright BP station, then a Burger King. *Ah, the christening of the West!*

Eventually, the grid-work of proper streets commenced and Morley, as he had on his first visit, marveled at the aforementioned "clash" of building styles. Gothic churches over five hundred years old stood side by side with 1920's rowhouses, no-frills '60s-style Communist apartments, and long sparkling black-glassed modern shopping malls (here, called "gallerias") that made even the fanciest malls in America look low-brow. Another delightful visual feature was thus: most of those old, drab Communist Bloc-era apartment buildings were now gaily painted with bright and vibrant pop art colors and designs. At any rate, the way in which this wonderful divergence of styles conformed to present a new vision of urban beauty was always something that had flagged Morley's notice indelibly. Add to that the city's overall immaculateness, and one found oneself in a metropolis of unique, impressive, and inspiring appearance.

But there was another trait which, to a man like Foster Morley, struck him as even more inspiring, and that would be the, uh, genetic...character...of certain of the *ferae naturae*, those of the female variety, that is.

In other words, the local women.

Here is where corruption—I'm afraid no other word will do— of this polite, highly cultured, and well-bred gentleman reared its head. Some might simply characterize Foster Morley as a man with a normal, healthy interest in members of the opposite sex as well as a normal healthy interest in discharging the instincts compelled by his sex-drive.

Yes. *Some* might put it that way. But most, I'm afraid, would put it another way: he was a sexist pig, an orgasm-addict, and a chronic "cunt-hound." When it came to the matter of sexual release, his articulate mannerisms and the intellectual presentation of his demeanor were but gloss, a well-honed veneer, beneath which existed a soul *percolating* with lust and with desires that would be described by any decent person as *deviant*. Elaboration on this point will soon be drawn, but it must first briefly be observed that Polish women were of a superior genetic stock. *That whole eastern European gene thing,* Morley reflected. Wherever his gaze might land, it was met with a pair of erect and often braless breasts that even the most persnickety would have to declare as indefectable. Anatomical delineations as of a centerfold's, legs like a runway model's, and eyes like... Well, this requirement of hackneyed similes intrudes well into this writer's capabilities. Mr. Morley's next thought, however, will allow the reader to visualize more clearly the images sought: *Dozens of them,* he mused, gazing through the cab's window, *everywhere I look, all drop-dead gorgeous full-tilt brick shit-houses.* Morley gently bit his lower lip, looking on.

That is, he gently bit his lower lip, and more than gently squeezed his crotch (the driver couldn't possibly notice) and reveled in that mysterious satisfaction which came to older men upon the sensation of pre-ejaculatory fluid escaping the end of the penis. It was an anatomical assurance that he wasn't all dried up just yet, something a man no longer young appreciated mightily. *Oh, my gracious! Yes, indeed, I am BACK in Poland!* he rejoiced, now noticing a statuesque young woman striding toward the trolley platform with both stupendous bare breasts exposed.

And how so this? Oughtn't there be laws prohibiting such lewd and unseemly displays of exhibitionism?

The answer is not far to seek. See, clinging to one large, wet, puckered nipple was the mouth of an infant, suckling nourishment in the manner which nature intended. Indeed, breast-feeding in public was not only allowed in Poland but also encouraged (and the same, too, in most of Europe), and this fact proved much to the benefit of infants and mothers alike. And also, yes, to voyeuristic perverts like most men, especially our concupiscent protagonist. However, the staid driver did not "bat" an eye: surely he was used to seeing such fleshly spectacles on a daily basis. Morley looked on with even more intent as their turning onto Swidnicka Street afforded a closer and more clarified angle of the event. The baby seemed to suck as if the mother's state-of-the-art breast owed it money. Milk dribbled from its tiny mouth, and the expression on the mother's face, as she strode along on her toned model's legs, gave every indication that she quite enjoyed the sensation of having her child suck her mammary glands dry. Morley looked on dreamily: *Oh, how I envy that child. If it's a boy, it's got a boner!* And it would be a weighty sum indeed that he'd pay for the opportunity to provide the necessary semen to put the *next* baby in her belly...

"Where to drop you?" said the driver without looking back.

"Ah, yes! Give me a moment; I have my confirmation right here," and then Mr. Morley fished through his carry-on until he succeeded in securing his print-out from Booking.com, along with the hotel name. *Ah, that's right. How could I forget a name like that?* Previous ventures to this city had shown him many hotels with similar names, such as Orbis, Ibis, Ebis, Elbis—evidently, or so he supposed, at least—the enterprises of a single management or holding company. He'd stayed at the Orbis on his first visit, set majestically upon a pristine, flower-planted hill facing an entrance to the Centrum, which he'd booked due to its history of being a diplomatic hotel in the days of the Communist Bloc. (Many supposed spies allegedly stayed there as well.) In all, his stay could not have been more gratifying with its clean, quiet rooms, a very polite and efficient house-keeping staff, and a wonderful bar and a menu which boasted the best smoked salmon he'd ever eaten (ah, of course, and also its convenient proximity to the best whorehouse he'd ever had the pleasure to enter).

But Morley preferred some variety on occasion, and as he'd stayed deeper in the Centrum during the last few days of his first visit; he'd put up at the Ibis (he believed an "ibis" was a sea bird of some kind—odd that there was no sea anywhere near Wroclaw, but what mattered that!) just as excellent as the Orbis, and this time, he'd picked the *Iblis* (note the "b' between the "i" and the "l", for the benefit of differentiation), obeying some inner monitor he couldn't quite identify. More than likely the choice was made due to the hotel's placement in an ideal walking distance between a wonderful Korean restaurant to the west (whose beef bulgogi and pork bukkum was as good as he'd had in Seoul), and, yet again, his favorite bordello westward—a ten minute walk in either direction, not more.

That, but might there be some other reason he'd chosen it sight-unseen? Soon after booking, he'd recalled from his college classes at Dartmouth that the word "Iblis" was stated as being the Islamic name for the devil in the *Qur'an*. Now, Morley was not at all given to occultism, but he did have leanings of interest in history, and this seemed a thoroughly unique hotel in which to put up...

Yes, a hotel essentially named "The Devil."

"Iblis," he intoned to the driver.

The driver glanced back severely. "Iblis?"

What might there be about the man's momentary change in demeanor? Morley could not help but notice it. "I have the address right here—"

"I know address," the driver half-grunted. "I take you."

"You seem—if you don't mind my mentioning it—to have had a negative reaction to the hotel."

"Huh?"

"Is there something the matter with the Iblis?"

The driver seemed to hesitate (or was it Morley's imagination?) "No, no," he gruffed. "Nothing the matter."

"Oh, I'm sorry, it's just that your bearing seemed—"

"Nothing the matter," the driver said more sharply. "Is just that Iblis is Polish-owned, but most employees they hire be Bosnians who do for less money. Same jobs, less money. Take good jobs from good Polish. At other hotels and restaurants they hire Ukraine for same reason. Then we have gypsies everywhere too, from Romany, all working jobs that should go to Polish."

At once, Morley comprehended the issue. The universal notion of national prejudice, countries holding grudges for injustices hundreds of years old, or more. "Ah, I see," was all he said. "We have the same type of thing in my country."

"And gypsies, Ukraines, and Bosnians," commented the driver further, "none are good Catholics."

Of course. Poland was nearly ninety percent Catholic, and... *I'm not exactly a good Catholic myself,* Morley thought, suppressing a chuckle. *I came here for houses of ill-repute, not houses of God.* "Well, I appreciate your information. I wasn't aware of these social anomalies here."

"Huh?" gruffed the driver.

Morley didn't respond further; instead his eyes opened in wonder upon noting the large, high sign and the nearly Gothic red letters on a black background:

IBLIS.

"Here your hotel. Iblis," announced the driver.

It was an interesting structure on the whole, and not depressingly new. Morley reveled in *old* hotels, because with their age came character and singular atmosphere. Not that it was vastly old, but old enough: a keystone at the arched granite transom read A.D. 1876. (*Was Wroclaw part of Prussia then?* he wondered. *Or the Hapsburg Dynasty? Damn! Some history buff!*)

The Iblis stood five storeys, a red-brick affair, and he thought sure most of the bricks were original. Clearly, Zhukov and his Soviet decimation machine hadn't bothered with demolition. There were, too, evidences of trimmings from late in the Gothic Revival period: small turrets and pinnacles on the roof, along with gray and grinning gargoyles. When Morley unseated himself from the cab, he felt certain he could look forward to a wonderful stay in an accommodation so "Old Europe" in appearance and nearly a century and a half old.

At the ornate front door, Morley waited for the stoic driver with his check-in bag. The delights of Poland were immediate: the 60 *zloty* cab fare all the way from the airport equated to 17 U.S. dollars. He tipped double that, for in Florida, the fare would've been a hundred dollars without tip. The driver nodded thanks blank-faced and seemed to return to his car and drive off in a hurry. This observation would've seemed foreboding, but our Mr. Morley was far too immersed in the experience of being here to notice.

As was his habit, he took time to visualize and therefore saturate himself with details for his travel "journal," which in truth existed as more of a journal of his sexual exploits rather than travel experiences (which he was determined one day to publish on Kindle, using a pseudonym, of course. Who knows? Perhaps even the author of this very narrative has published such a book...)

Through the outer front doors, he found himself within a small, well-adorned glass-and-brass vestibule, no doubt installed to intercept cold air blowing directly inside during winter. But as this was *not* winter, the second set of doors only succeeded in cutting off airflow from the lobby, and this observation is being made for a transitive purpose: someone else stood in the vestibule.

For some reason, Morley had not immediately noticed this.

Our traveler was at once accosted by a high, whiny male voice warped by some derivative of accent that cannot be effectively reproduced via the written word; it sounded like these words, rapidly spoken: "Give me five euros, five euros, five euros!" and with each outburst of "five euros," the stranger's hand was thrust down and opened.

Morley was not suited for sudden confrontations, and his offense was trebled by the unignorable presence of the odors of a human being unwashed for weeks and staggeringly soiled clothes.

Morley perceptibly gagged.

The stranger, of course, was no more or less than a common beggar, of which there was no shortage in Poland. This beggar however, was atypical in a number of ways, and a few words must be expended upon this point.

This malodorous stranger stood no taller than four and a half feet, yet didn't seem to answer to the description of someone affected with dwarfism or achondroplasia. Unkempt jet-black hair in something of a bowl-cut adorned a relatively normal head; his skin tone was the hue of, perhaps, peanut butter; and a partly Asiatic face was heavily populated with pimples. Yet the most notable anomaly next to his height were the evidences of severely foreshortened arms—clearly half the length one would expect for someone of this height—perhaps a nine-year-old boy. This person was handicapped, of course, disabled, and ordinarily our Mr. Morley's heart would've gone out to the poor chap, but between the appalling smell and the shock of his rude vociferations, Morley admitted to himself that loath, not pity, was what most significantly seized him.

"You *American!*" came the next gust of foul breath, which

was backed by decayed teeth. He'd said *American* as if it were an indictment. "You *rich!* You give me five euros, five euros, five euros!"

Morley at last composed himself, or at least as much as he could. "Sir," he replied, trying not to gag outright. "There are ways for the disadvantaged to ask for money, and there are ways *not* to. You have demonstrated the latter method," and then Morley pushed himself and his bags through the next barrier of doors while simultaneously a hotel security guard, who'd noted this event, muttered an apology to Morley, yelled at the vagabond, and banished the small man out onto the sidewalk. Morley slid away, not cut out for this sort of imbroglio. The guard spouted more invectives, then closed the doors. The beggar glared as he struggled back to his feet, but he wasn't glaring at the guard.

He was glaring right at Morley.

Back inside, Morley thought, *Gads! I cannot abide unpleasant confrontations! And the poor bum is looking at me as if his expulsion were my fault!* But one thing Morley was expert at was insulating himself from the after effects of such encounters. It was an unfortunate mishap—the world was full of them—and Morley (especially at his age) determined to let nothing spoil his enjoyment of every living moment, and the incident was nullified at once as he opened his eyes to sumptuous decor of the lobby as well as opened his lungs to its unsullied air.

A lovely, homey front lobby greeted Morley's gaze. Dark, ornate throw rugs of considerable size adorned the hardwood flooring: carpets more like tapestries, stitched somewhat in the technical style of England's famous Bayeux Tapestry. Certainly theses rugs warranted further study, for even in that first glance, Morley spied depictions of figures of nobility and also figures of warfare, such as rows of grenadiers, pikemen, and musketeers; fat cannons belching smoke; and even, more unpleasantly, executions via firing squad, torture, and hangings and decapitation whose visual expressions of victims proved to be the work of no unskilled needle. (Had Morley examined the rugs with more scrutiny he would likely have noticed other depictions even more graphic and disturbing, such as soldiers raping headless women, whose severed heads seemed placed deliberately to look on, nude women being boiled alive in great black vats, and still more nude and very despairingly faced women being impaled on sharpened pikes from mouth to vagina, while some military spectators were actually depicted to be masturbating. Indeed, not an exuberant display of needlecraft, however technically expert.)

Who would put such an obscene and gory carpet in a hotel? he wondered. But more than likely, however, only the hyper-normally attentive, such as Morley himself, would even notice such minute and barely discernible details.

Certain lobby furniture and gilt-framed paintings struck him as Oriental, while other such stuff—evidently newer furniture and paintings—were clearly fashioned in the Arabesque tradition. This might've affected the common traveler as an incongruence, an eyesore even, but not so our Mr. Morley. Like the overall outside urban clashes of architectural styles, he found this clash of interior decor to be unique and unrepresentative—just another interesting "feather" in this city's "cap."

A glance to the left showed him the double brass- and glass-doors to the hotel's bar and restaurant. A stoop-shouldered elderly man pushing a vacuum cleaner cast him an errant look with a deadpan face like the taxi driver. When Morley briefly studied the menu posted just outside the door, he noted cuisine that seemed Chinese as well as Polish, along with some other entrees unfamiliar to him. He very much looked forward to dining there.

At last our visitor advanced to the front desk, a bit out of breath from the weight of his luggage and his encroaching age. Across the brightly lit counter, a dark-haired young woman with razor-straight bangs and a shapely figure offered an enthusiastic greeting. "Oh, hallo, sir! Welcome to Iblis! Would you be Mr. Foster Morley?"

"Why, yes," he said, and presented his ID and booking information. "How did you know?"

"Hotel is full except for one room, yours, sir."

This was clearly a good sign, while another feather in the aforementioned cap was that the desk clerk looked quite a bit like the Spanish actress Penelope Cruz. In fantasy, Morley couldn't help envisioning himself ejaculating on her nude body from "naves to chaps" (which meant, according to Shakespeare, from navel to neck.)

Oh, what a luxury that would be, he thought.

She returned his papers and said, "We hope you will find satisfaction here, sir."

I suspect I will, he answered in thought, *but not quite the satisfaction of, say, the sensation of my dick between your lips.* Instead, he just said, "Thank you."

"You are room 12, on second floor. And here is—" she slipped him a business card with the hotel's name and logo—"wi-fi code. Is free."

"Superb, thank you." His brain was lit up with the pleasures that awaited. And he couldn't wait to get situated, turn on his laptop, and scan the most recent entries on the "Odloty" website that seemed to be the best call-girl website for Poland. Then he remembered something: "Oh, and if you will—where is the nearest place I can convert U.S. money? The galleria across the street, I suppose..."

"Oh, no, sir. Is a changer right here, open until 1700," and she pointed to his left past one of the bizarre paintings.

Shit, he thought, *1700, what is that?* Some slow, feeble calculations in his head told him it translated to 5 p.m.—ten minutes away. "Pardon me, I'll be right back," and he rushed away down the short hall, and it was only then that he noticed the peculiar color all the lobby walls were painted.

Blood red.

Morley's brow furrowed. *Probably not the color I would choose for MY lobby,* but then it was uncharacteristic and therefore interesting. No matter, he furthered himself down the short hall and found the exchange window, behind which was a small cubby fronted by glass like a bank teller's. He expected to find a curmudgeon of a fat old woman behind the window but—no!

Another young raven-haired beauty smiled behind the glass. *Would you look at the tits sticking out on this one!*

"Hallo, sir! Welcome to Iblis," she said, her accent contorting the hotel's name to "eee-bleese."

"Your words of welcome are much appreciated, and it is my

pleasure to be here in your beautiful country."

She stalled, then said, "Oh, Poland, yes. Poland is a much lovely country, yes, but I come from Bosnia, also much beautiful."

Interesting. The cab driver had said as much, with more than a little resentment. She must be here on a work visa. "I'll have to visit there sometimes. And now, if you could kindly change this into *zlotys*." From his wallet, then, he extricated one thousand U.S. dollars, a hefty wad. The attendant's eyes widened, then she deftly counted it and produced an even larger "wad" in Polish currency. "Tharty seee-ven hundred farty," she pronounced.

Morley restrained elation in deference to good taste and respect... but the dollar had strengthened since his last visit—and when the dollar strengthened—a good thing for Morley's wallet—that meant that the *zloty* had weakened a bit. "Thank you very much, young lady. And this is for you," and he slipped her a tip of 100 *zlotys*.

Her face lit up; she gushed, "Much thanks, sir! Very much thanks!"

Morley nodded with a smile, then turned to embark back to the front desk. However...

His eye snagged on one of the strange, gold-framed paintings, apparently an original oil, not a print. The elaborate framework depicted a bust of a nobleman, in a dark red tunic with tight collar, and a headdress which struck Morley as absurd: a puffed up orb like a fully cooked Jiffy Pop, only gold instead of silver. Dark intense eyes, a thick straight moustache, and a fearsome facial expression were the subject's most prominent features.

A small engraved brass plate at the frame's bottom read MEMED II.

Only a few seconds' thought brought him back to his Dartmouth European history lessons. *Yes! Memed II was the ruler of the Ottoman Empire, whose army sacked Constantinople and finished what was left of the Roman Empire.* But this odd recollection induced him to question the even odder portrait. *What the HELL is a painting of Memed II doing in a hotel in Wroclaw, Poland?* Constantinople, then renamed Istanbul, was over a thousand miles away from the charming Polish city in which Morley now stood.

Hanging a picture of an Ottoman sultan who'd slaughtered

Europeans with the ferocity that the Americans had slaughtered the Indians made as much sense as a Japanese hotel hanging a picture of Robert Oppenheimer.

And if the reader will believe me, Mr. Morley was incapable of putting "two and two" together for another full minute of contemplation…

Of course! Memed was Muslim and so are most Bosnians! Bosnians just might regard such a man as Memed II as a hero…

A curious consideration, yes, especially since he remembered what the cabbie said (with more than a little derision) about an influx of Bosnians working for lower wages in Polish hotels, particularly *this* hotel. Might the Bosnians working here have secretly mounted this rather inappropriate painting?

Interesting speculation, he thought with a jovial twist, *but frankly useless! I don't give a SHIT about Memed II or Bosnian immigrants or anything else! I'm here to get laid!*

Back at the counter, he received some final information from the attractive clerk (the nature of which I don't know), and then pocketed his key with thanks, hefted his bags, and made his way toward the elevators.

Elevators in Poland are habitually slow, perhaps, or perhaps this one was an exception. I am not sure. But Mr. Morley contends that he waited at least ten minutes for his ascent to his room. The majority of these minutes was spent in his examination of the guttering fountain and goldfish pool. Morley smiled into the pleasant display which adorned the area.

This smile, however, transposed to a grimace…

Oh, dear, he thought.

The gold fish were of the kind one often sees in Chinese restaurants: the *hana fusa* variety, seemingly the *ugliest* variety, covered with bulbous growths inclined to remind one of tumors. These, however, were especially unique. But how so?

All of the fish in the display floated belly-up and…headless.

A macabre image it was, to say the least, and not much of an enticing decoration, but in fact it was a bit funny, and without any conscious prompt, the following words began to construct themselves before his mind's eye:

Oh, where, oh where are the goldfish heads?
Oh, where, oh where can they be?
He went to the water to make a wish
And found a school of headless fish!

Had not the elevator just then yawned open, I'm afraid quite a bit *more* terrible poetry would have been laid before the unfortunate reader...

Mr. Morley stepped in to accept the elevator's invitation, he set his bags down, then heard something *clink* behind him. He turned and noticed he'd dropped his room key. So, naturally, as would anyone, he stepped back out to retrieve it, and halfway through the arduous process of bending over, heard the elevator doors clatter closed.

Oh, what balderdash!

He immediately poked the door button, thought, *with my luck it's going all the way to the top before coming back down,* and then watched the lighted indicator reveal the elevator was indeed going all the way to the top before coming back down.

Then another thought occurred to him. *What if my bags are no longer there? What if they've been pilfered?*

He did not like the stead of *that,* but his frets were for nothing, for when the elevator again returned, there were his bags, just as he'd left them.

It seemed strange, though, that no one had stepped off the elevator when the doors reopened. *Probably a servant traveling from the fifth floor to a lower one and disembarking before the car had come all the way back down.*

As the car next rose slowly to his floor, rather noisily, he recalled the odd case of the headless goldfish. The answer occurred to Morley in a flash: *Either there's one very big fish in that tank that I didn't see—and with a mightily full stomach—or there must be a very happy cat in this hotel!*

Further rumination kindled his thoughts (it was a *very* slow elevator) and it struck him how fortunate he was that his bags had not been stolen. In, say, Russia, Brazil, or Morocco they most assuredly would've been, but Poland, like Denmark and Sweden, was not a country known for thievery. His carry-on bag, in fact, housed a knapsack-type tote that contained his $3000 laptop. *Lose something like that in Europe, and it would be hacked in hours and expunged of all passwords, account numbers, etc.*

Once arrived at Floor 2, he trudged out of the lift, then, seeming to recollect himself, examined the pointer signs which indicted the direction he must take, and next, we find him standing before the brown door for Room 12. The hallways were painted the same unnerving blood-red as downstairs, but now he was starting to warm up to the color's richness and seeming dimensionality.

No card-keys here—in fact he'd never seen them in Poland; supposedly they rotated the door locks when someone checked out (at least, he certainly hoped they did!) Much jiggling was required to coax the key into cooperation, and in just a smidgen of time he had effectively transferred his bulk through the door into the room.

It was a modest room but also deserved the epithet of "cozy," for the tan enamel walls worked well with the mahogany-brown door and window trim, and the tone was restful without being dull. The comforter on the king bed boasted this same brown, and so did the curtains of the room's only window. A plain brown dresser faced the bed, topped by a 30-inch-or-so television. (Incidentally, of all his journeys abroad, our Mr. Morley had never once turned on a hotel television. Why spend lavish sums to travel only to point your face at inane American reruns that weren't even in English?)

A cursory glance at the window showed him a wide brown embrasure, many small panes, and a rather dismal view of a wide alley, lined by the rear of another hotel more modern and, I must say, *less* engaging to look upon than the Iblis.

Not many words need be expended on the bathroom, save to say it was quite like all European hotel bathrooms: white porcelain tilework, sink, toilet, and inadequate mirror, and a stand-in glass shower compartment the size of an old-fashioned phone booth. The only picture of note on the wall was a watercolor print of the city, dated 1929.

And that was the tale of the room, for any interested in details.

A fine room, to say the least; Morley had no need for staggering opulence in a mere hotel room in which he clearly wouldn't be spending most of his time. He could afford it of course, but such luxuries seemed superficial and not efficient. No, the lion's share of Morley's wallet would be dealt *outside* of the hotel, where he hoped to be spending more of his money—and semen.

With a huff he hoisted his large suitcase onto the commonplace strapped trestle found in nearly all hotel rooms, and this he opened in order to commence with the task of arranging his clothes in the closet in apple-pie order. Several pairs of pants on hangers in hand, he approached said closet, reaching to pull open its brass knob, but stopped, feeling a curious and clearly unpleasant shimmy in his gut...

An untoward sound seemed to be emanating from *inside the closet.*

All of things...

Identifying this sound came easily enough: it was the sound of someone snoring very lightly.

This is preposterous, he thought. *There can't possibly be someone SLEEPING in my closet,* so he put aside his hesitations and opened the closet.

From the floor, a wan face looked up, clearly in horror. The eyes opened so widely they appeared lidless, and the mouth held open in a silent scream. Morley noticed at once that the interloper was a young woman, dressed in the white blouse and black blouse of the hotel's staff, and there was another feature of note: *Jeez! Tits-a-Million!* Of the three women he'd encountered so far in the hotel, *this* one's breasts were the biggest. Morley's half-flaccid member bumped up a notch with this recognition, and with that bump came another drop of anticipatory ooze.

"What's the meaning of this, young lady?" he said, trying to sound authoritative but failing utterly. "This is my room, rented and paid for with my own money, if you will. I must say, that if you've used a pass key to get in here, I—well, I certainly don't approve. What can possibly explain my finding you asleep in my closet?"

The young woman began openly to weep and very ignominiously crawled out of the closet. Morley was discomfited by this image of subservience (he may have been a pervert and a sexual exploiter of women, but he *wasn't* a callous prick!) and he—with effort—bent over, took her arm, and helped her to her feet. "Up you go, missy. There, that's better, isn't it?" and the action of her rising inadvertently brushed her hip over his crotch. *Ooo!* he thought. *Almost let one go in my pants with that!* "Sit down on the bed and tell me what this is all about."

She seemed to understand, and her eyes, damp from tears, fluttering incessantly. "My name eese Andela—"

Morley was taken a bit aback. "Why, what a lovely name, and one I'm sure I've never heard before!"

She either ignored the remark or did not fully comprehend it. "Yes, sir, I do use pass key to come in and sleep but did not wake up. You see, they here break the law, they force us to work twelve hours or more without pause, which eeze *against* law. I work so far tharty-five hours with no sleep or break. This they do so they no have to hire more girls, just make us do it all and no overtime."

Morley, at once, was appalled (however, not *so* appalled that he took his eyes off her mind-boggling bosom). He took her hand, "Oh, you poor child! That's nearly slave labor! Is there no Better Business Bureau in Poland? Aren't there qualified authorities you can tell?"

"No, no, sir, you don't understand." She hitched a few more sobs. "If I go to police, I not be believed, and they send me back to Bosnia."

Morley's brow rose. *Ah, yet another Bosnian.* But now the young woman's dilemma was clear to see. She'd stolen into his room to get some sleep, since the managers wouldn't let her go home...

"That's quite terrible to hear, Andela," he said with sincerity. "I'm very sorry for your misfortune."

But now the pretty woman was sobbing outright in what seemed cataclysmic terror. Still sitting on the edge of the bed, she leaned forward in a lurch, hugged Morley's hips where he stood, and cried, "Please, please, kind, sir! If you tell managers I was sleeping in your room, I get fired and sent back! So bad I need this job, to send money to my children and family in Bosnia!"

He wondered what percentage of the hotel staff might actually be

Polish. But to the girl, whose nonchalant proximity to his crotch was causing a bit of a stir, he said at once, "Oh, my poor dear girl, is that what's upsetting you? Well, have no fears. I promise you I will not tell anyone of your being here, and believe me, I quite understand your hardship in this matter, poor child."

The woman quivered in a relief that was very nearly convulsive. "Thank you, sir, thank you much! I am so afraid of being sent back home!" She hugged him tighter now, with the side of her face pressing full against the front of his pants.

Oh, dear, he thought. Morley was quite sensitive to his situational weaknesses, and as much as he fantasized of unhousing his member right then and there, and "slaking himself of hand" right onto her face...he knew he mustn't misbehave; after all, he was in a foreign country. *Discipline,* he calmly told himself. He gently nudged her shoulders back, and helped her to her feet. "Up you go, young lady, and there's no reason to be upset." He gave her a tissue from the box on his desk. "Dry your tears and have no worries. Now, if I understand you correctly, your shift ends in an hour's time, then you can finally go home for a good night's sleep. So run along now—" he slipped his hand in his pocket and withdrew a stray bill. "Here's fifty *zlotys*—no, I see it's a hundred. Take this, with my good wishes, Andela."

Saying that the girl was beside herself by the gesture was a severe understatement. It was as though she'd never seen a charitable act in her life; she was actually shaking. She hugged him, "You the only nice man I ever meet." Her whisper in his ear turned hot. "I must thank you," and then she slid down his body to reseat herself on the edge of the bed.

Before he could finish saying, "Andela, it's not necessary to thank me," her hot, small hands were already busily cosseting his crotch through his trousers, fingers defining the shape of his growing penis beneath the fabric. Morley's head swam, and his sphincter went tight. Further protestations were overruled by a quick "Shhh!" from the girl, and then the zipper came down, and it was all out right in front of her face, and his shaft was hard and thumping in less time than one could say "holy shit!" Some minuscule filament of his upbringing suggested that he was taking advantage of a poor, desperate young woman in the midst of her travails, and that he should push her head away and end this inexcusable exploitation right here and now.

Ah, but, no. Our Mr. Morley did nothing of the kind.

A small, hot, wet mouth admitted quite deftly Morley's penis to the "root," and then in an action that could nearly be called "studied," Andela's lips tightened in a meticulous slowness while the very tip of her tongue feathered over his glans. Soon the girl's lips had sealed about his shaft like a rubber O-ring and began to, in a rather mechanical fashion, draw back and forth, minutely gaining speed. A few minutes of this and Morley's knees were shaking, and all that built up angst from looking at three flights worth of European flight attendants and every manner of international preposterously attractive female traveler during three layovers in three big airports...well, all that imagery and now this on top if it had Morley on the brink of an orgasm that was fit to burst and subsequently release enough sperm cells to populate an entire planet. Quite abruptly, however...

What in the name of Pallas...

—Andela's ministrations ceased.

She looked up at him with a salacious grin, held a finger up to denote that he should pay attention, produced from seemingly nowhere a condom packet, and put it in her mouth. Her eyes remained locked on his as her closed mouth moved around in the oddest manner, and in a moment the empty condom packet was ejected between her lips. *Amazing!* thought Morley, his dick beating ludicrously in front of her face. Next, that same dick was swallowed once more by the girl's mouth and suddenly the rubber was on it.

Andela stood up in a flash, pulled off her panties concealed by her skirt, grabbed Morley by the collar, and flung him onto the bed. She kneed up over him, holding up the skirt to brandish beautiful loins darkened by a shiny black pelt of hair—none of this worn-out faddish shaved business—and sat at once on Morley's aching, thumping erection. But she did not locomote her hips up and down as one would expect; instead, something moved up and down *inside her* in the most unique sensation. No doubt Andela's vagina muscles were as adroit as a gymnast's. What was the official anatomical designation? The *Kegel* muscle, or some such? Well, whatever might it be, Andela's..."pussy" was sucking Morley's cock as adroitly as her mouth had been previously, while she barely moved her hips at all.

"Ah, *fock!*" she panted. "You have very best cock!"

Some fairly ridiculous gasps and exclamations escaped Morley's lips—sounds that even the most experienced novelist could not possibly reproduce with the written word. His body seized up, his mouth gaped like a just-caught grouper's, his eyes bugged, and out pumped his orgasm in a series of wild, excruciating pulses. By the feel of it, the ejaculation was voluminous enough to call "formidable," especially to a man of Morley's age. Ah, but as other sounds might imply, he wasn't the only one orgasming.

Andela seemed to be experiencing seizures right then and there, writhing violently, such that Morley worried at first she might be epileptic, but a moment later he worried that she might be demonically possessed by the way her back arched, and the way her eyes rolled back in her head. But, no, she was just having a climax, which evidently was a good one thanks to the proficiency of Mr. Morley's erection. That deft Kegel muscle of hers spasmed away and constricted with such tension it almost hurt...not that Morley was complaining.

Next, with a great smiling sigh, the girl went lax atop him.

It occurred to him that he should say something complimentary to her but he found that he lacked the wind in his lungs to utter anything. With an effort, he rolled her off of him and sprawled, tongue out, sucking in air, fish-out-of-water like. But Andela bounced to her feet, all smiles and bright eyes, and righted her clothing. She offered him a naughty look. "Oh my gosh, was best orgasm in my life!" and she'd pronounced it as *argism*, which struck him as terribly erotic. "Oh, let me," she said, taking a visual note of something.

Morley, of course, could take no visual note of anything just then, save his bulbous belly and the ceiling. His knees shook when the girl's hot little hand squeezed his deflating penis, sending a final remnant of semen down his urethra and into the rubber. Then, in a devilish slowness, she slid the rubber off, twirled it till it corkscrewed down to a band, squeezing its contents into a sphere at the end, and held it up for him to see.

"Watch, now!"

He might have known by now, but the girl put the entire thing into her mouth...

Morley's eyes bugged.

He thought she meant to swallow but—no! Her closed mouth moved awkwardly for some moments, and next...

She ejected the used prophylactic into her opened palm, then held it up by its end when it swayed in the manner of a pendulum. It had been tied into a knot, in her mouth.

That's some parlor trick! Morley wanted to applaud and would have were he not so thoroughly exhausted. He'd seen women do this trick many a time with maraschino cherry stems but, but—

A used rubber? Now THAT'S what I call talent!

She dropped the business into the waste can by the door, then giddily leaned over and kissed him on the lips. "Much thanks to you, sir! You are wonderfulest man I ever meet! But now I must go, I must sweep lobby!"

Morley's hand raised to wave and his mouth moved to say goodbye but, alas, he'd still not regained enough breath. The door clicked shut. And there lay our Mr. Morley: his pants down, his dick out, and his belly sticking up like a soccer ball under his shirt. He was content to remain like that for several minutes, so sated was he, and so gratified to have provided the poor girl a fine *argism*. Next, he fell asleep.

Whether he fell asleep just like that (i.e., pants down, dick out, belly jutting) or not, I don't know, and I didn't ask. I am simply recounting the story as he told it to me. When he wakened, the room was filling up with dusk, so, given this was only the first night of the many he had at disposal, he settled on delaying his visit to Klub Krystal—his aforementioned whorehouse of choice—until "the morrow," as the British say, and that would allow him to shower, have a meal, and perhaps treat himself to a short perambulation about the regions of the City Center that might be in a more convenient propinquity. *Why rush?*

And if truth be told, the much needed sexual release of earlier left him feeling a bit drained—in more ways than one. He chuckled at the thought: *My girls at the Klub will have to wait a bit longer for the attention of MY John Thomas. You see, I have it on very good authority that my prowess as a love-maker leads to the best argisms a woman can experience! There's only so much of me to go around, eh? I'm not a piece of meat, you know. I'm a human being, damn it! I have feelings too! Nobody wants me for anything but sex! I'm just a great big fuck dummy!* And then he laughed aloud, to such an extent that he could feel his "man-tits" jiggle.

First, he would shower, and in order to do this with any regard to practicality, he must first unpack, so to have ready clean clothes to don. He rose, pulled up his pants, heaved his Samsonite onto the bed, and opened it.

He froze, then, at an unexpected observation...

Now, this the was very odd thing indeed. When he'd opened his suitcase, a scent—er, no, an *odor*—eddied up. It wasn't particularly strong but it was unpleasant just the same.

The odor was undeniably of *fish*.

This had happened once before, as he recalled, when traveling from Oslo, Norway, to Venice, Italy, by way of Frankfurt, Germany's airport, known as Rhein-Main-Flughafen, (and you can trust me when I say that there are good airports in which to experience long layovers, and there are bad ones; Frankfurt is among the latter in this category), where a twelve-hour layover was necessary. You see, back in Olso, he'd inadvertently placed a small packet of prepared sushi—in a clear plastic box—into his luggage. Such imbecilic gaffs were rare in the life of a man as orderly minded as Morley...ah, but of course, he *was* getting older, and his brain and metabolism took longer and longer to adjust to the jet-lag as each golden year ticked by. All that aside, the mistake was made, and this he recollected only after arriving at his Venetian hotel the next day, when necessity compelled him to open his suitcase...

Same smell here, right in the face: fish going bad.

Mr. Morley stared puzzled, for he was certain he'd not made the same blunder twice with regard to carry-out sushi; in fact, he'd *had* no sushi anywhere in weeks.

Morley's fattish fingers rifled through the small suitcase's content, but they didn't rifle for very long.

Gads!

There, beneath the second neatly folded (and rather expensive) Thomas Mason dress shirt lay...a ground up "plop" (about the size of a golf ball) of some glittery, silverish, orangish...*stuff*, and our protagonist—if that he be, really—found himself thoroughly incapable of identifying it. He resorted to his pants pocket, summoned his handkerchief, and then after a pause induced by the vague but repugnant smell, picked up this-this...*plop* of...stuff.

It was wet; this he could discern by feeling the moisture seeping through his handkerchief. To the bathroom he took himself next, rather in a some haste, for Mr. Morley (as was often his wont) found himself in quite an incontrovertible state of perplexion. The bathroom's bright CFL bulbs beamed down, and Morley found himself, in close scrutiny, examining a small mass of something organic that had clearly been masticated (i.e., something *chewed*). Tiny protrudements of *bones* seemed evident, then something like— of all things—a very small fish mouth.

Lastly, a minute eyeball with a gold iris looked back from the chewed mass—

Abominable! thought Morley. *Absolutely abominable!* for it took our traveler far less than a moment to put two and two together this time, and realize that this wet plop of stuff comprised the *heads* of the goldfish whose decapitated bodies he'd seen floating in the decorative pool downstairs by the elevators.

Morley's face pinkened in outrage. Obviously, the "fish-headchewer," whoever he might be, had seized the opportunity for this awful prank when Morley's baggage had traveled up and down the elevator without him, earlier. It was true, Americans were sometimes the victims of pranks of "hooliganism" in Europe, but not so much in Poland, a land very much developed with high-levels of civility. (In Germany, France, and England, *not* so very much.) Be that as it may, this outrage must be reported, and Morley determined to do that as immediately as he could manage, but...

Was there something else?

Oh, yes, indeed, there was!

A much more pressing priority than reporting the fish-head incident was thus: checking the Odloty website to see if his favorite girls were still members of the staff at his treasured Klub Krystal. Out came the laptop, on went the desk lamp, and *plop!* went his fat ass into the chair. His emotional excitement swelled as he waited for the computer to start, and so did...something else, as he let his mind be filled with thoughts of the triad of delightful harlots who so wonderfully serviced him during his visit a year ago. *What were their names? Ah, yes!* Nikolina, the raven-haired. Katreen, whose red hair was so light it was almost blond. And Essie, the pouty-faced brunette with the cocked hip and sly grin—Morley's personal favorite.

My girls, my girls! he moaned to himself. *I'd row a league for any of you!* but of course this was abstraction. Our Mr. Morley was too old and fat to row a single stroke. However, just that errant thought of the three girls raised Morley to "full mast" in his pants. *What I wouldn't give to be eighteen again. I'd have this bad boy out and spilled on the desk in two seconds!*

Now, as he waited STILL for his blasted Windows 10 to get on with it, he pictured each of the three prostitutes more precisely in his mind, in macro-photographic sharpness. First Nikolina, tall and slim and wide-hipped, the straight-black hair down to her waist. She was modest-bosomed and very tan, and wore a choker, a headband, and a braided rope belt, but absolutely nothing else—*like a haughty Woodstock tramp*, he thought. But Katreen was anything *but* modest-bosomed; she was the brick shit-house of the three, but a *tiny* brick shit-house, for the top of her head came barely to Morley's sternum. *And her tits?* he thought and whistled. *Tits sticking out so far you could lay out Thanksgiving dinner on them.* Her most salient feature (at least to a sexist pig like Morley) was the clitoris protruding like a fleshy pink nose from the shaved-bald pubis. Morley had reveled more than once sucking this Tootsie-Pop-sized nugget of girl-meat. Of course, performing cunnilingus on international prostitutes couldn't have been more unwise in this very virusy day and age, but Morley's view on the matter was along the lines of, *Fuck that! You only live once.*

Next, of course, was Essie...

Merely the sound of her name in his head issued an instantaneous throb of drool in his trousers. Essie boasted a sturdy body, breasts like cupcakes of white flesh with dark-pink bon bons atop them. Like the others, she, too, was shaved bare without a trace of stubble, proffering to any viewer a pubis that meant serious business, a Hit-It-Like-A-Champ pussy; indeed, a feminine cleft that begged "Beat Me Up... If You Can." Most arousing about this specimen, however, was her overall visage: narrowed eyes and a cunning grin just barely showing teeth—it was an absolutely *vulpine* look—and her common stance, always feet apart, one hip cocked, and one or both fists on hips. Were her aura able to speak, it would say "I will suck you dry and fuck you 'til you're sucking your thumb and crying for your mommy."

Blast...

The thought of these girls, especially Essie, had him squirming in his seat now, hard as a piece of polished cherrywood, and hornier than a hyena full of spanish fly, and he was only a moment away from extricating his member from the strictures of his pants and calling on the attentions of Rosie Palmer right then and there, and—

Let this interruption be regarded as an amusing aside, but one that Mr. Morley had conveyed to me with some jovial concern a few years back: that he confessed to quite a bit of paranoia whenever circumstance forced him to *masturbate* in a hotel room. He could not elude the idea—unlikely as it was—that all such rooms of accommodation may well be fitted with *hidden cameras* to provide the hotel staff with entertainment. Secretly watching an attractive couple make love could be regarded as entertaining enough, appealing to the voyeur in all of us. Ah, but how much *more* entertaining would it prove to be secretly watching a lone fat man nearing sixty engaged in the act of taking himself in hand in the manner of the Old Testament's Onan, second son of Judah who was slain by God for spilling his seed in a non-procreative manner. That notion would frequently nudge its way into Morley's mind whenever trying to "huff one out" on a hotel bed. Fat man, stomach sticking out, fist desperately shucking up and down over a penis barely visible due to the big pale hairy belly; the other hand clutching a scrotum constricted to near non-existence, man-tits jiggling away, squirming, face twisted up like Shemp in the Three Stooges, struggling for the orgasm that always seemed to take a little longer to achieve. Morley could picture the little office someplace where hotel staff sat clustered around the video screen watching the debacle, *howling* laughter. This observation, of course, has nothing whatever to do with the story but it is mentioned here to shed more light to interested readers on this one little oddment of his mind-set and self-image.

Now, back to the story, where we find our Mr. Morley just about to un-trouser his erection and go to town, when—

"What is the name of..."

His pants, indeed, remained zippered, as our protagonist stared aghast at his laptop screen. You see, it was at that precise moment that everything booted up, but it was very much *not* the familiar Windows 10 Desktop.

It was instead the most vile and horrifying spectacle he'd ever espied on a computer screen or anywhere in his life for that matter—which had somehow come on by itself. And it was no more or less than this:

A naked woman, well-nourished but not fat, with her hands lashed behind her back and, on her knees, is being forcibly bent over a filled bathtub, screaming. Two men are in attendance, both naked, lean, and well-muscled, and both wearing transparent Halloween masks that do not reveal their identities but only show the most vague suggestions of humanity beneath (if indeed any real humanity remained.) The first man holds the woman's head below the water; the other kneels behind her, evidently sodomizing her with a prodigious erection. The camera must be suspended overhead, for it points down, offering a Kubrick-like point-of-view. From this abhorrent angle, Morley can not only hear the unearthly sound of the woman screaming underwater but can see her *vomiting* beneath the surface. The visual effect is...interesting and akin to nothing Morley (or probably anyone else) has ever seen. The woman's mindless thrashing in the water, after a time, ceases. The man to her rear finishes his sodomy, then lets her flop out of the tub, whereupon he pounds his fist against her bare chest repeatedly. The girl's body quakes, then a great spatter of water ejects from her lips, and she begins coughing maniacally. The two masked men celebrate their resurrection by high-fiving each other, and they laugh and jabber in a foreign language. Then they kick her and punch her senseless. Next, the woman howls animal-like when the first man punctures her eyeballs with what appears to be a screwdriver. Both men, now, pick her up and drop her right back into the tub, then step away from the spilled water on the floor. Neither man now can be seen—only the blinded, beaten woman who thrashes in the tub, screaming, coughing, and howling.

Suddenly there comes a splash.

From somewhere out of the frame, something sails, then lands in the tub. A clock radio? A hair dryer? An electric can opener? It doesn't really matter; whatever the object might be, it is clearly connected to a live power cable. The tub along with its contents seem to *surge*. Popping, snapping, crackling from exploding sparks merge with the woman's screams, which by now sound unlike anything that could possibly be generated by human vocal cords. This crush of madness, motion, and sound ensues for another minute, until at last, the woman goes still and dies for the second time that night. The thrown object—obviously unplugged now—is hauled out of the tub (a hair dryer, after all), and then the two masked stars of the production re-enter the frame, drag the dead woman out, and begin raping her again, all the while chuckling with an echoic effect...

Our Mr. Morley tremored in his seat, slack-mouthed and with peeled-open eyes. He was visibly shaking. Multiple questions marauded his brain at once, like a machine-gun burst, all too fast to be comprehensible. Now, just exactly what the thoughts were, I don't know; at certain points of this narrative, I can only epitomize what he conveyed to me upon his return, and harness my own speculation and creativity. But I can discern that he was much troubled by this video clip; moreover, how was it so that the clip was on his computer in the first place? Why had it come on when it had, with no command from Morley himself? A worse thing to wonder was whether the clip depicted was real or staged. He hoped for all he was worth it was the latter. And if it *weren't* staged?

Then I've just watched a snuff film, came the chilling realization.

Evidently, the computer's built-in video player had come on by itself, but why would it do that? A glitch? The possibility seemed feasible, but Morley was *not* a computer whiz. He knew how to turn it on and locate files and programs, but that was the limit of his expertise. The most pressing question, of course, was the evidence of the video file itself. It was certainly nothing he had procured himself; a pervert he was, yes, but *not* the kind to interest himself in subversive stuff such as this. Moreover, if the clip were indeed genuine, its very nature made it felonious, and no doubt mere possession of it would qualify as a serious crime—an *international* crime, since he was a foreigner. Either the clip had been loaded via some virus (Morley *was* known to surf dubious sites at his leisure, and he knew that dubious *European* sites were particularly notorious for highly complex modes of malware; perhaps he was being naive in assuming that his anti-virus program was impenetrable), or someone unknown to him had installed the clip purposely.

He did not like the prospect of that.

But solving this queer mystery took a deep back seat to the expeditious removal of the file.

For fuck's sake! he thought. *I'll have to search the entire hard drive for the file, and I have no clue how to do that!*

One of Morley's chief faults, however, was overthinking and therefore overlooking details of any dire situation—certainly a fault which worked out well for him just now. He'd forgotten to look in the most obvious place.

In the tiny slot on the computer's right edge he found an SD card where there'd been no SD card when he'd last touched the computer.

Morley removed the card. It was black, as were most of them, but there was no label. Logic insisted that he destroy the card at once and do away with it.

Ah, but Morley was not the most logical of men.

He fell prey to the most irresistible urge to see if the file had a name, and weak as his computering skills were, he knew how this was achieved. He replaced the card into the slot, opened the file manager, and clicked the drive designated to SD card. A single word popped up on the index:

VRACANJE

A Polish word, obviously, and one he was wholly unfamiliar with. He should have attempted an online translator but something else caught his eye which seemed more pertinent. To the extreme right of the index was a figure which indicated the size of the file: 14GB.

Even Morley knew what that meant (fourteen gigabytes) and he knew, too, that it was an uncommonly large file, at least enough to fill three DVDs. Mere deduction made the next calculation for him: that the first abhorrent segment he'd seen comprised only a fraction of the entire file. And as you may already have guessed, our protagonist now exercised some exceedingly poor judgment, and turned the video player back on to see what else might be on the card.

This was a big mistake.

There were more video clips, many more. First, a very short clip, seemingly rather old; perhaps it was a digitalization of an old black and white film. A young naked woman lay in a bathtub, tied up with dog chains. Gagged, she churned in the empty tub, bug-eyed, while a nondescript man stood aside and, first, urinated on her and, second, masturbated on her, but the lighting could only be described as poor, and the dead silence and grainy film quality lent a ghostly quality to the spectacle. A full minute flickered by, then two more men appeared and in an almost perfunctory manner, they carefully upended two glass bottles (each about a gallon) into the tub. The clear fluid looked like water but...it wasn't. Fumes thick as smoke billowed, and the captive convulsed and flipped and flopped as of a fish on a hotplate. Several more bottles were dumped in, and soon the fumes obscured all, a blessing. Finally the men turned away, revealing to the camera faces covered by gas-masks. The fumes billowed and billowed.

Next, in a shocking contrast, another clip followed in bright, stunning resolution, high-saturated color, and Dolby sound: several nude teenaged girls in an empty cement basement shrieking like broken flywheels as a pack of obviously starved pitbulls were released on them. One dog was gnawing a girl's face off while another dog was gnawing out the bare crotch of the same girl. Meanwhile, the largest dog, presumably the Alpha male, had already eaten out another girl's innards and was now attempting copulation. It was Hell gone mad: the combined sounds of machine-like shrieks and inexorable snarling, gnawing, and gulping, and the way in which the dying girls twitched, disemboweled, some insanely flung up fleshless forearms in useless defense, one dog wagged its stump tail as it as it pulled another girl's breast off, stretching it like a rubber tug toy, and all the while, that Alpha male still vigorously copulating a corpse.

Morley may actually have cried aloud as his finger darted forward to turn off the video but in his haste clicked the wrong button and only forwarded the clip to the next selection, which appeared to be turbaned and black-masked terrorists, in broad daylight, reveling as they watched an industrial-sized garbage compactor slowly crush to death several dozen living people amid the chant, "Allahu Akbar!"

No no no! Morley's thoughts screamed, *No more! Turn it off!* but his hand shook so badly that he again clicked the wrong button and was now watching still more—this time, not a crowd of black-masked Al Qaeda or Isis but simply a scene in the woods. This scene, unlike the others, displayed a time-stamp: 15:13 (3:13 p.m.) and date of something just under a year ago. The camera wobbled as booted feet of the videographer were seen advancing across the leaves of the forest bed, and crunching sounds accompanied this, but judging by the sequence of the sounds, at least another member followed along.

Birds chirped gaily, and continued to do so even when the party stopped and the camera focused on the target of its mission.

It was a girl, a young girl—clearly a *dead* young girl. Yet the camera did not linger enough to provide more details; instead, it homed in on the decedent's face: bloodless, yes, but peaceful, even serene. Strawberry-blond pigtails lay splayed off from her head. Though death had closed her eyes, she merely looked asleep.

One man in the party knelt near the head, and as if in a magic trick produced a straight foot-and-a-half long knife with a wooden handle, quite similar to the carbon-steel sashimi *Usuba* knives seen so often at Japanese restaurants. They were the ultimate fish-cutting knives. This one, however, would not be used for cutting fish.

With great finesse, the kneeling man began to skive away the dead girl's face, sloughing off strips of very pale skin in the tradition of an apple peel. The subtle sound of the blade working—*skritch, skritch, skritch*—caused the blood in Morley's head to drain; he nearly keeled over. The girl's lips, nose, and cheeks were quickly removed and flung aside, until only the lidless eyes stared upward. Then the bladesman began to whittle off the forehead skin, and then the scalp.

When Morley was able to recompose himself, the scene had changed. Another man leaned into the frame, which meant that three persons were present for this little onus, as the camera remained aloft. The man leaning down brandished a pair of shears and—*snip, snip, snip*—cut off the dead girl's heather-blue summer dress, then her white cotton panties. There was no bra, and Morley saw next that none was necessary, for now, as she lay naked, her physique revealed only the tiniest buds for breasts, a hairless pubis, and no real evidence of hips— in other words, the victim was a child who couldn't have been older than ten years of age. *"Pierdolic trupa,"* came an unseen male voice, and now this second man, too, knelt, after parting the girl's white legs, and from unbuckled pants he displayed a stout, throbbing erection. Meanwhile, the face-skinner kept cutting, and this was when Morley let out a dreadful moan and removed the SD card.

He later made the allusion to me that, like Poe's un-interpretable "The Man in the Crowd," wherein the story does not permit itself to be read, the remainder of this video segment did not permit itself to be watched.

He may have passed out for a time, from the trauma of what he'd seen on his laptop, for it was several hours later and already dark when he next became fully aware of himself.

He needed something to disengage his mind and this was it: the Centrum or City Center. But this was no Rodeo Drive or Park Avenue full of tinsel, phony people, and over-stated "hip" architecture; this was a cultural and mercantile nexus whose labyrinthine byways were formed by buildings far older than America. He accounted the Centrum as one of the most intriguing and beautiful places he'd ever seen in his life: a living, moving spectacle, and more beautiful still in evening-time, when it was all lit up.

Eventually his sentience surfaced from its previous mortification, and he found himself showered and dressed and out on the street, walking swiftly away from the Iblis and up toward the glittering lights of the Centrum and all its hustle and bustle. The city's nickname was "The Meeting Place," and Morley easily saw why. Even this early in the evening droves of friends were converging to form various clusters in which enlivened conversations ensued and shortly thereafter, each cluster headed en masse to the agreed-upon restaurant or bar.

To his left, he passed a favorite eatery, The Sphinx, which specialized in roasted meats of all types with a Middle Eastern flair for spices—the barbequed goat ribs were especially delectable. To the right, he then passed the Literatka café, a famous tavern for local writers and artists, and where Morley frequently visited for the Pilsner Urquell draft beer and post-modernist artwork. But tonight Morley stopped in neither establishment, walking instead in something of a fugue state straight across the Centrum's main square, passing the ancient Rynyk section, various bronze statues of noteworthy Poles, and the infamous Glass Fountain, which was quite beautiful in spite of the locals condemning it an eyesore.

Deeper into the Center, a labyrinth of vendor's stalls commenced, selling everything from handmade cheese and honey, to "Slinkies" of fried, spiral-cut potatoes, to a plethora of smoked meats and jerky, including rabbit jerky. Coffee, tea, and beer stalls, too, abounded, and more stalls of exotic jams, jellies, and marinades, and of course the stream of moving shoppers navigated each lane, abundant with staggeringly attractive Polish women.

Ordinarily, our Mr. Morley would've purchased small samples from many of the stalls, and his eyes would surely have feasted on the myriad of lovely women, to imagine the exquisite flesh beneath their apparel.

But not tonight.

He didn't even notice the great City Hall, built in the late 1400s, nor its exemplary astronomical clock; these were normally sights Morley delighted in. His fugue state drew on as he walked, and he supposed part of his conscious self was closing off his normally excited power of observation in order to push back from his senses the horrors he'd seen on that video clip.

The next thing he consciously recognized was where he seemed to be heading: the cobble-stoned path which eventually led to *Ostrow Tumski* (the Cathedral Island, home of the Cathedral of St. John the Baptist and the Church of the Holy Cross, among the city's two most celebrated churches). But Morley had little interest in churches, nor spirituality, and though he did possess an enlivened interest in old architecture, he had already seen these two particular churches in the past, and had no desire to see them again...

So why was he walking here now, seemingly in a trance?

Then the strange word appeared in his mind's eye: VRACANJE, the word hand-written on that atrocious SD card.

God in Heaven... Morley thought, nauseous again.

But now it occurred to him why he'd bypassed all of his favorite city's main attractions to come to Cathedral Island.

The river around the island was the nearest body of water.

It was then that Morley's subconscious mind released his true intentions: he meant to dispose of the card as irretrievably as he was able. A common garbage can wouldn't be good enough, nor would a sewer drain. He needed to *see* the card disappear forever beneath the flowing murk. *Out of sight, out of mind,* he mused, but with little satisfaction. Of course, his first idea had been to take the card at once to the *Policja,* but only a second's reflection nullified the idea. That card was a digital storage device full of snuff films, child pornography, torture, rape, and God only knew what else. Mere possession of such horrific contraband was no doubt extremely penal. The police would want to know exactly how such a thing had come into his possession, and what would he say? *Well, officer, you see, someone infiltrated my luggage, put the card into my laptop without my knowledge, and—oh, and they also deposited a mouthful of chewed up goldfish heads into my suitcase.*

No. Our Mr. Morley was not going to say that.

And it was well-known that the Catholic Church, whether directly or indirectly, had its hands in a little bit of everything in Poland, including the criminal justice system. For the data on the SD card, Morley could easily find himself in prison with a hundred-year sentence. *Can't afford to fool around with this stuff. I'm a foreigner in a foreign country with no Bill of Rights.* Therefore, any civic duty there might be in reporting the card to the authorities would have to be ignored.

He noticed stars twinkling in the twilight between the two grand cathedrals just as he stepped on the famous steel footbridge that connected the Centrum to Tumski Island. The bridge was "famous" because it was known as Lovers Bridge; for over a hundred years, lovers had been etching their initials onto padlocks, locking them to the fencing along the bridge, and dropping the keys into the water below. A touching sentiment, for sure, and many European bridges had the same sentiments.

But when the bridge was clear of pedestrians, it was no key Morley dropped into the water, it was the SD card. He even heard a tiny *plip* as it hit the channel's surface. *Good riddance.*

Worrying about how exactly the card found itself in his laptop slot would only do more damage to his mood than the card itself. But anyone would regard it as the most obvious question: who had secreted such an atrocious thing into his computer? Moreover: why?

Our Mr. Morley was perhaps a bit reclusive but he was first and foremost a good person. He doubted that he'd ever had an enemy, and couldn't recall a time he'd treated any other person with any ill will, rancor, or contempt. He was a pleasant man who strove to keep everything pleasant about him, and this was how he'd always been.

I'm sure it's just national prejudice, he considered. *The Ugly American—me. Fat, rich, extravagant.* It was true: a majority of Europeans didn't like Americans for the same reason most of the rest of the world didn't. *Higher standard of living, more freedom, less unemployment, more Starbucks, more food, more movies, more gadgets, more everything.* It was human nature: blame your problems on the people who have more. *Somebody in the hotel slipped the SD card into my computer when my luggage went up the elevator. Just to freak me out. Have a laugh on the rich fat guy. Well, to Hades with them! That card is lost forever, and I won't let anyone besmirch my joy!*

And so it went. Morley crossed over to the bustling, well-lit island. He gazed out past the cathedral, fixed his eyes on the glimmering, murmuring River Oder, then turned right around and headed back to the Centrum. Food, drink, and perhaps some *sexual release* was his idea. It was the perfect way to forget all about this bad start to his vacation.

Another thirty-minutes' perambulation took him, in a rather cursory fashion, about the Centrum's nooks and crannies—always a pleasant and scenic venture, more especially as nighttime slipped closer. He passed several grocery stores, which reminded him that he must soon purchase some smoked salmon; not only were the grocery stores here cleaner and much better stocked than those in Morley's homeland, but the smoked salmon in Poland was vastly superior to any he'd had anywhere in the world. But he decided to make that purchase on the morrow when he could go to his favorite grocery, the Carrefour Galeria Dominikanska, closer to his hotel. Next he passed Empik, a fascinating art and magazine store, and next, Fenick's, the multi-story department store where he'd been known to purchase underwear and other clothes rather than suffer the tedium of finding a laundromat. Irresistible aromas chased him past Soho Café, another must-stop location, because the chicken livers and onions simmered in butter and the roasted pig knuckle were staggeringly good. Many signs invited him with the welcome word *Alkohole* but this too he resisted, as much as he could go for a beer now.

By now he'd wandered close to the Centrum's perimeter, passing the KFC (and, yes, the chicken tasted better here than in America, just like everything else), and the ZuHu strip joint (once notorious for putting "roofies" into the drinks of unsuspecting foreigners and robbing them). Miles in the distance he spied the Sky Tower: a famous tall black obelisk-like high-rise of luxury apartments, with a swanky shopping mall at its lower floors. This mall housed Morley's favorite sushi bar in Europe, the Fuku Bistro, and they even stocked Japanese beer, but it was too far a walk tonight. He passed the great bronze statue of Boleslaw the Brave, Poland's first king, and one of the most imposing statues in the city. Here began the outer sector of Swidnicka Street, a main thoroughfare, and that which would navigate him to his intended destination.

But first, nature called.

It occurred to him now how much better he felt since he'd put aside his ruminations regarding that confounding and ultimately *evil* SD card. His first night here was being salvaged quite nicely. At last, he found the sought after sign—*toaleta*—and entered in haste.

Here was just another example of why he so appreciated the civility of Poland: public restrooms much cleaner than those in his homeland. When finished with the chief business at large he, of course, washed his hands, and as the water rushed from the faucet Morley caught himself for an odd moment staring disconnectedly into the mirror. His brow furrowed and he froze, and then the image of his face seemed to warp and wobble as if in a wide ripple of water. Some unidentifiable impulse locked Morley's gaze on his own reflection and refused to let go—er, well, not *exactly* on his own reflection, but just beyond it, into the area of space over his shoulder, behind him. *What in the DICKENS am I doing?*

Then his eyes began to tear up in the sudden wake of the most awful odor—an odor dense as fumes—and at once his stomach began to quake. At least if he was going to throw up, he was in the right place. Had he more of a creative bent, it might have occurred to him that the appalling smell could be likened to that of a human crotch unwashed for weeks—or, no, ten or twenty such crotches concentrated at once. Morley wobbled where he stood, fought off several more urges to vomit, turned off the faucet, and was about to rush out, but something he glimpsed in the mirror froze him in place: behind him, low, and to his left. It was a face, a brownish face pocked by acne, and spiky short jet-black hair. Rotten teeth blared through its grin.

Then Morley remembered: the short, short-armed "bum" who'd accosted him for money in the entrance of the Iblis. And now, yes, he remembered the stench, that atrocious body odor that made his eyes cross.

"You!" Morley shouted, "I remember you!" and with a bravado I do not think is common to him, he spun around to confront the interloper. "You swarthy little bugger! You're stalking me! I've a mind to call the authorities," but there was nothing to be seen once he'd fully turned, only the rapid patter of footfalls, a chittering chuckle, and a more intense waft of body odor.

Morley was not fit enough to give chase, of course. He percolated in place for a few moments, sorting out his aggravation. *Let it go,* he advised himself. *What on earth would I tell the police? Excuse me, officer, but there's this very short, brown-skinned man with terrible acne and unduly short arms who has seen fit to harassing me, because I refused to give him money earlier. And by the way, he smells quite bad, like— well, quite like an ass crack...* No, that wouldn't do, they'd think him an idiot. He prepared, then, to leave, and be back about his business, but when he approached the rest room's exit, another observation stopped him in his tracks: it was a graffito, scrawled either in red marker or lipstick on the light blue tile wall.

It read: VRACANJE

* * * *

Cut to the chase, our Mr. Morley thought, and now walked much more forcefully down Swidnicka Street, passed the spacious Renoma shopping mall, then the Arkady tram stop where he had once nearly been run over for not paying attention and actually "shit" his shorts a tad. It was dark now, but the little treed courtyard through which he walked glittered with pleasant, twinkling lights. Several beggars had tactically presented themselves, and they were all of a much more amiable turn than the invader in the toilet. Morley dispensed money to them without heed—one man was actually standing on his head, and for no short time. All of them gushed thanks in multiple languages.

Again, his mood was uplifted after the previous unpleasantries, and now his pace quickened under the starlight. Lights up ahead seemed to boom as if announcing his return to the long row of shops, cafes, and bars that existed immediately beneath the overhead railroad bridge, a street with the inconceivable name of Wojciechutzkitba. He felt lost in a happy time as a train chugged by at that moment, rattling; his eyes scanned the row of taverns and shops, all familiar to him. He was especially pleased to see the Sielanka pub, a favorite of Morley's. It was appointed with early 1900s furniture and wallpaper, not to mention stolid-faced portraits of Polish businessmen from the days when Poland didn't exist. And Morley spied with delight the Primator sign on the window, Morley's very favorite Czech "piwa" or beer. And on he walked, heartbeat rising with each step. Three more storefronts, then two, then one, and then—

Outraged *blared* into his face.

Oh, heartbreak of heartbreaks and horror of horrors! his thoughts bayed. *It can't be true!*

Morley's mouth hung ludicrously wide. The storefront that had just one year ago boasted Klub Krystal, the best whorehouse Morley had even entered, now boasted no such thing. Brown clumsily painted doors now showed these words: PUNJABI RESTAURCJA OF INDIA.

Fuck! Morley thought at the limit of his capacity for profanity. *Those motherfuckers shut down my whorehouse to sell INDIAN food? I came here to eat Polish pussy, not tandoori chicken!*

Morley stood there staring for what was likely many minutes, his face lengthening and lengthening as the truth laughed back at him. No more Klub Krystal. Gone. Pushed by western commerce into non-existence. The anticipation of the past few minutes' walking had even compelled a feisty erection, but down it went now, down, down, down.

The storefronts on either side were outdoor taverns, and a fair share of the patrons had begun to take notice of Morley—all in a manner that suggested his behavior might be deemed irregular. *Hey, everybody, look at the fat American staring at the restaurant that used to be a whorehouse!* It occurred to him that he may even have moaned an utterance from the shock of this crushing verity. Finally, though, his consciousness gave him a jab, suggesting he move along before his anomalousness might attract the *Policja.*

But wouldn't you know it?

Just as he turned to leave, the crappy looking brown doors swung open, an exotic female silhouette appeared before a thick gust of curry scents, and the words trumpeted: *"Ciesze sie, ze wróciles!"*

Morley squinted, suspecting his imagination was toying with him but—no!—the woman in the doorway was none other than Essie, Morley's all-time favorite prostitute!

"Essie!" he exclaimed. "My prayers are answered!"

The pert young woman wore a purple chiffon **sari** as would be the fashion in India (but clearly *not* the fashion in Poland). She fairly flew off the front steps and collided into Morley, embracing him like a long lost love. "I do not believe what I see when first I look out window! But eeze true! My American is back!"

Yes, my dear Essie, he thought. *I'm back, and HARDER than ever...*

Next she was yanking him by the hand—"You come, you come with me here!" and next they were nearly stumbling through the front doors and into a small dining room sporting paintings of Lord Krishna and the Shiva and Shakti, patterned wall coverings in sedate ochre tones and pastel pinks and blues, an obligatory model display of the Taj Mahal. She urged him deeper, into a darker cubby toward the back, and here Morley noted the cozy aura overall that was projected by the candle-lit tables and calm sitar music, and—oh! But why do I encumber you with such trivialities? Mr. Morley didn't "give a shit" about the restaurant and the authenticity of its decor. He only cared about one thing, and he was looking at it.

"Essie, my gosh! What happened to Klub Krystal?"

She frowned. "Bah! Ice-hole owner go in jail for no paying taxes. That fock us all up bad. Nikolina, and Katreen go away to Warsava, hoping for other hoo-er place like Krystal. Me, I stay. Thought I might be homeless, was going to join fockin' Polish Army—bah! Can you see that? Whole army would be using me for fock-dummy first day!"

No, Morley could *not* see that, nor did he care. *All I care about is this wonderful piece of ass in my arms!* He squeezed her harder, rubbing his burgeoning groin against her stomach.

"So then I meet *new* ice-hole who build theese sheet restaurant," she continued, "he offer me job if I suck him off every day and swallow—bah!—but I agree, so I wait tables and wash deeshes. Fock! Indian food is such *sheet!* I get free meal every day but never eat, and every night I go home, I smell like *fockin'* curry! Yeck!"

Morley tried to be polite as possible by showing genuine interest in the woman's travails, but this turned impossible after another moment standing there embracing her. The heat from her body through the sheer gown was killing him, as were the soap scents in her hair. He could not prevent his hands from delving beneath the sari-gown and shucking those delectable white cupcake breasts out into the open. The visualization rocked him, and so did her sudden sly grin and chuckle.

"My dearest, sweetest Essie. What you must understand is that I am in dire need at this moment. I simply *must* be with you, now, this minute," Morley insisted.

"Huh?" she responded, but of course, her English wasn't the best. Instead, the universal language of lust deciphered his words when her hand slipped into his pants and toyed with what throbbed there. "Oh, eeze like bar of iron!" she whispered. "You want for me take care of it, hmm?"

"Yes, yes!" Morley gasped, hugging her tighter. He lowered his mouth to a nipple and sucked it like a baby sucks its mother.

"That's my big American boy," she purred. "You suck that teet hard, and tomorrow I *fock* your American brains out—"

Morley straightened up in panic. "Tomorrow? Great ghost of Ariadne! I need you to fock my American brains out *now!* Right *now!*"

Her vulpine grin sharpened, and her eyes thinned as she viewed his desperation. "No, no—tomorrow it must be. You must be— what's word? Patient, yes! I must work here now in theese sheet restaurant till twenty-two, then wash fockin' deeshes till midnight and run to catch last train home."

Another avalanche of disappointment; Morley couldn't abide the thought of not having her tonight, of not having her luscious warm body spread-eagled beneath him and that sly lascivious grin looking up at him. He was so deliriously aroused just then that he couldn't let go of her, he simply couldn't detach himself. Essie chuckled under her breath, all too familiar with such helpless anguish. She widened the part in her *sari*, to cruelly afford him a last glance at those succulent bare breasts, and then she wrapped them back up. He was trying to dry-hump her where she stood, and this only made her more aware of his desperation. *Damn this!* he thought. *It's not right!*

Her hand in his pants felt around more concisely and then marauded his constricting testicles and gorged cock—a merciless tease. "You be good American boy and keep theese deek hot for Essie tomorrow." Then she withdrew her hand, which caused Morley to groan in a manner that was—he declared— *mournful.*

She finished fixing her *sari,* then gave Morley a paper card. "This my phone number. You call me tomorrow noon. I have all day off from theese sheet place, so I will fock you all fockin' day and suck your deek and make you cum so much you won't need to cum again for a fockin' year."

Morley nearly came just from hearing her say that, in that sharp zippy erotic accent. Her presence was making him dizzy, along with the clear fact that there'd be no coupling betwixt the two of them tonight. Then a bell over the front door jingled, signaling customers. "I must go now," she said. "You call," then gave him a peck on the lips and turned.

Dejected as he may have been, a thought struck him. "Oh, Essie? I have a question."

"Yes?"

"What does this word mean in Polish?" he asked and quickly wrote VRACANJE on the back of her card.

Essie squinted; her bare shoulders shrugged. "I know no word like theese in Polish."

Then off she scurried to the several diners who'd entered. Morley, now a personification of human dejection, sidled himself around the group of customers and slipped out of the restaurant unseen, as if he were virtually non-existent.

The moon hung high now, a bright white beacon shimmering down over the Centrum. The public gaiety he'd so noticed earlier seemed to have doubled by now: happy groups and couples all bar-hopping and making the scene. Lots of laughter, lots of big bright smiles. Here was a sparkling, joyous society indeed.

Ah, but poor Morley could not be part of it; he was the odd man out, the loner whoremonger. In shifting visions, he tried to picture himself as a member of one of these happy groups but it was impossible to form any such image. *I'm just a wretched, isolated old man who can't fit into society without a fistful of cash. Without money, I'm the invisible man...* The half-daze he'd experienced when leaving the hotel re-occupied him now, but, if anything, he felt more distant. All the brightly lit open spaces of the Centrum were filled with even more people, but our Mr. Morley felt much further away. The collision of opposite emotions made him wince: the devastating disappointment of failing to arrange a tryst with the voluptuous Essie, along with the outrageous, throbbing sexual arousal ignited by their brief contact. *This is driving me crazy,* he thought in the most excruciating anguish. *If I don't jerk one off soon, I may disintegrate...* The image of Essie's body, especially those bare white breasts shucked out of the *sari*—it nearly brought tears to his eyes as he walked past the KFC and all the circular benches populated by smiling, hand-holding couples. These feelings were just more icing on his dejection.

But when he tried to direct his mind in another, less unhappy direction, the effort unsurprisingly failed. Essie had been unable to translate that bizarre word on the SD card—*vracanje*—which only compounded his confusion and melancholy. One thing he'd always markedly enjoyed about the Centrum at night was the way which its bright yellow lights created an artificial daylight. Now, though, he scarcely noticed it, and it occurred to him that the entails of his vacation thus far had proceeded so poorly that full depression had set in. *Maybe I should just go back home tomorrow...* The idea seemed worth considering; even as much as he loved this city, many things weren't right this time, starting with that ghastly SD card and his unpleasant run-ins with that deformed beggar. *Gads. What a disaster this is becoming.* How this atmosphere could depress him—the bright lights, the exuberant couples, and the vibrant art nouveau adornments to the surrounding architecture—it was all beyond Morley; it seemed that there was some kind of odd joke on him.

He supposed he should probably eat something, and here he was now passing the famous and very medieval-looking Piwnica Swidnicka Restaurcja. Opened in 1246 A.D. in the basement of the Old Town Hall, it was the oldest restaurant in all of Europe. The thought enlivened him: *I'll go in and have a big glass of Okocim Lager and a plate of Pirogis!* It seemed just the remedy to this oppressive funk.

Ah, but when it rained in Mr. Morley's life, it *poured.* A Polish/English plaque on the huge front doors confronted Morley with the unwelcome notice that this once-lauded restaurant was no longer in operation and had since been converted to a historic building. Morley's face lengthened at this information, then, like a weary automaton, he turned and trudged away, resigned now to the day's utter and irreversible failure.

So...

On he walked, past the famous Whipping Post of Old Town,

where thieves were flogged skinless for stealing as little as a single grape; past the ancient church whose spiring heights hosted The Bridge of Doomed Maidens where, at certain times of night, one may see the wraiths of forlorn women who were never blessed with matrimony, and past the well-known Hansel and Gretel Houses and the baroque archway that joined the two. Here, Morley stopped for a moment of perusal. Morley was aware of the pair of houses by means of a tour guide last trip: two thin, five story tenement houses built, it was said, in the 1500s and fortunate enough to survive the Soviet wrath of the War. They had nothing to do with the cannibalistic Grimm fairy tale but received the moniker from their charming Bavarian style. The words MORS ET VITA IN PORTA were engraved over the arch. *Should be easy enough*, he considered, taking his mind back to the basic Latin of high school. *Let's see. This should be easy enough. Mors—that's right enough for death. Vita, obviously life. And porta...ah, yes, gateway. That's it! Death Is The Gateway To Life.* But after a few moments' thought, Morley didn't like the stead of that. It seemed too grim *Hmm, well, it must be some religious axiom: only by dying can one ascend to Heaven. At least I hope so...*

Beyond the arch—the "gateway"—stood a church, but it was now too dark to see; and around that assortments of small shops, but all closed now. Some impulse seemed to be goading him to walk through the arch; however, he resisted the impulse. Though crime was low in Poland, only foolhardiness would allow an obviously well-heeled foreigner to wander about such unlit alcoves at nighttime.

Next, he glanced down at the walkway which proceeded under the arch. It was attractively distinguished from the rest of the Centrum's square brick tiles by being comprised of *hexagonal* tiles which led all the way through the arch.

And beneath these tiles?

Morley knew the stories from the guide books. Centuries ago, a group of anarchists had risen up, burned some buildings in the square, and taken over the Town Hall, then the governmental seat. But before they could make their demands, the military had raided the building, escorted the governor to safety, and then killed many rebels on sight. But a dozen ringleaders were spared for trial, which had issued most expediently. All were found guilty in a court of *oyer* and *terminer*, and were branded in the town square, flogged on the wooden horse, and then beheaded for all to see. Those dozen bodies still lay buried beneath the hexagonal tiles on which Morley now stood.

A charming tale, indeed, but history had never answered the obvious question:

Whatever became of the heads?

Morley chuckled at the query. Like most legends, it was probably sheer fabrication or at the least exaggerated. He took a step forward, then another, and stopped. Then a voice floated out of the archway's dark maw: "Hey, you. You know theese place, eh?"

It was a rasping, somewhat corroded voice, but distinctly female. Morley felt a jolt in his heart when a figure did indeed surface in the archway's darkness. Of course, it was a beggar, a bent old lady in a hood and cloak. *A gypsy, no doubt,* Morley supposed. "Good evening," he said.

She nodded and shuffled forward, showing very few teeth in her smile. "Aha, eet eeze, very much so a good evening. Every evening good when alive."

Morley chuckled. "I agree, and I share your optimistic attitude."

"Seeing you English, do you know story here?" she asked, pointing down at the hexagonal stones. "Theese place here?"

"Yes, I believe I do. Traitors were executed for an uprising, hundreds of years ago. Their heads were cut off and their bodies buried under these tiles, the poor buggers."

The woman extended a wrinkled finger. "Aha, you know! You smart!"

Another chuckle. "Well, it's in the travel guides."

"And you know what they did with heads?" the old woman grinned.

"No, madam, I do not."

"Ah ha, so now I know something you don't know"—here she nodded, and Morley could guess what was coming next—"and if good American man please be kind to give ten *zlotys* for food, then I tell."

For Morley, "please" was the magic word, and besides, he liked the poor old woman. She did not verbally assault him as the so many of the beggars here were wont to do. And what she asked for was a pittance, only about three dollars. "My dear woman! Ten zlotys will buy very little food, I assure you, *very* little. Here, this should be of benefit," and he gave her 200 *zlotys*.

The wizened face in the hood lit up. "Ah, *tak*, I know first I see you, you good man, and may God be upon you!"

"And you as well," Morley said, but he was getting a bit impatient. He really wanted to know. "The heads? What happened to them?"

It was almost like a cliche the way she raised her ancient finger and said, "Ah! The heads of those *lajdakies*. They be thrown by the soldiers into city garbage pit—ah!—but next day were *gone.*"

Morley knew the game, and this time he wanted to play. He was very much enjoying the woman's hyperbolized conversation. He gave her another one hundred note.

She caught her breath, and looked at him with the knowingness of a grandmother. "Good English man, what you give to poor come back to you ten times."

"So I've heard, madam. But, please. What happened to the heads?"

Her wrinkled eyes narrowed and she leaned forward, and she stood in a long pause. The old woman certainly knew how to add suspense to a story! "The heads be taken in middle of nighttime...by *czarodziejs*—"

"By whom? I don't know what that means," Morley hastened.

"By *devil* men!"

"Oh, I see. Satanists or something of that sort, I presume..."

"And they put heads, all twelve, in forest where they can be seen this day."

"In the forest? Which forest? And why put them there?"

She nodded in the hood, and for a moment a cut of the yellow light over all the Centrum caught on her face to disclose how very very old she was. "In forest behind Dominikanska," her voice rasped. "Eeze *haunted* wood, *cursed,* for all time since Adam."

Dominikanska? How marvelously intriguing! It was the big

shopping mall just across from his hotel, and there was indeed a forest behind it—he'd walked in it himself just a year ago to see the thousand-year-old brick wall he'd read of in the travel books.

"But why put them there, of all places?" Morley asked. "What purpose did these devil men have by doing that?"

But the gypsy ignored the question and again raised her wrinkled finger. "But good English man, hear me well. *Never* go to these woods. *Never.*"

"Oh, ma'am, I've not intention of doing so, rest assured. But please tell me why the devil men put the skulls there."

"Your aura *ill* now," she said.

This was getting aggravating. "What? My *aura?*"

"English man, please go back where you came. This place not for you..."

Her cloaked form began to recede back into the shadows.

"Madam, please! You *must* tell me." He extracted another hundred-*zloty* note. "I *must* know! Why did the devil men put the skulls in the woods?"

The old woman's outline seemed to go in and out of focus, and she never came forward to receive the note. "There to scrape the skulls," her ancient voice grated.

"Scrape?"

"See, skulls of wicked very powerful, and more powerful when put in cursed ground. *Czarodziejs* scrape skulls for corpse potions."

Morley squinted. "For corpse *what?*"

By now the woman had receded fully back into the darkness beyond the archway, but before she disappeared altogether, she said this: "For *vracanje...*"

Morley's eyes bulged. "Wait!" A jolt of adrenaline shoved him forward in pursuit but then he froze stiff; better judgment forbade another step. The sheer *blackness* within the archway seemed to churn as of a living mass of some manner of malignity. *Damn it...* More mystified than ever now, Morley gave up on the idea of following the old gypsy, and walked back to the Iblis Hotel.

* * * *

After such a convoluted and even terrifying day, Morley needed to feel comfortable, and there was no better place to achieve this than in the hotel bar. He felt a hundred years old when at last he settled his bulk down on the padded barstool. Behind him, the long, narrow dining room was about half full, and redolent with the aromas of Chinese cuisine (much more to Morley's liking than Indian aromas). An unsurprisingly gorgeous young woman tended the bar, with bright eyes and a beaming smile, and the silken dark hair he'd seen on every woman working here. She'd brought him a plate of egg rolls and a half-liter of Pilsner Urquell, which he thought of as the most reliable pilsner in the world.

Better, he thought after a sip. *Much better...* Finally he was starting to unwind from all of the day's frazzles and kinks. The restaurant stood nice and quiet, and the Chinese guitar music was a perfect touch because it so low as to be completely unobtrusive. Morley felt his aging body relax in stages; it was a nice, placid feeling. Even nicer was the view when the barmaid, ever smiling, began to wash glasses in the sink that was located right across the bartop from where Morley sat. Every time she bent over to rinse a glass, of course, Morley was afforded a bird's-eye view of the girl's white, creamy cleavage.

Indeed. Things were *much* better now; he was finally feeling like himself again and, yes, his aggravated penis began to stir. First the tortuous tease from Essie and now this, these, these... *Awesome tits*, he thought. Down she went again, to rinse another glass, and each time she rose, she smiled at him. Was she doing it on purpose?

What did it matter? Being in Poland was like being in a spectacular art gallery: everywhere you looked, there was a new work of art to feast your eyes on.

By now he'd discarded the idea of leaving early. Why? Because he had a bad day and someone was pulling pranks on him? *Balderdash*, he decided. *I'm staying and I'm going to have a marvelous time*—this thought as he delved deep into another glimpse of the bar girl's cleavage.

And next came the enlivening contemplation: *And tomorrow I'll get to do more than look!* Essie had said she was off tomorrow; she'd given him her number. Though Morley was hardly proficient in using a phone in Poland, he could have the front desk dial for him. He couldn't wait to bury his face in Essie's smug, teasing pussy. *I'll show that wonderful, sassy bitch just what an old man can do, and I'll plow her like a fuckin' potato field!* The thought scintillated in his mind and his crotch. Another sip of pilsner, then he withdrew the paper card she'd given him. Even her handwriting of her number was sexy. *Fuck...* But then he errantly flipped the card over without much attention, and saw the word he'd jotted down for Essie to examine: VRACANJE.

The word on the SD card, and the word the little deformed man had written in lipstick in the john, and, yes, the same word uttered by the gypsy woman before she'd disappeared in the archway.

When he looked up from these thoughts, the barmaid was rinsing another glass and, either by accident or design, her white blouse had come open by another button, and now the flawless white flesh of her breasts were showing some nipple-edge over her bra. *She's GOT to be doing it on purpose,* he reckoned, *and if she's making a play for ME, well, I must say she's picked the right guy!*

"Pardon me, Miss, but maybe you can help me with something?"

Her eyes beamed. *"Da?"*

"Do you know what this word means?" and then he gave her the paper card.

Her head tilted when she saw it. *"Šta je ovo?* Why you have theese?"

"Oh, its just a word I saw on a wall."

"Eeze Bosnia word—"

"Is it now? How interesting!"

The pretty girl squinted. "Eet mean—how do I say in Engleesh? Umm, deviltry? Yes, or *witchcraft.* Mean witchcraft."

Finally, the definition was upon him, and as he thought on it, it was none too surprising, with all the gypsy woman's talk of "devil men." "That's fascinating," he remarked, but there he went again, letting his eyes drop to her cleavage. This image, along with that of Essie's bare breasts sticking over the Indian gown, left Morley's penis at the mercy of his hormones. He was leaking aplenty a moment later. *Not this again! It's simply maddening...but in a good way!* If only she would proposition him, then the business would be all the easier but that wasn't likely to happen, or—

No! Perhaps he was mistaken...

Now the girl leaned closer to him. "Could you help me please with something, sir? I must get box down from shelf but I not enough tall."

"I'd be delighted," Morley said and stood up at once. "Lead on, my dear."

She briskly escorted him around the bar, down a small corridor sporting several doors, then led him into a cramped storeroom, which she immediately closed with her rump. Morley began, "So where is this box you—"

"Shhh!" came her fierce whisper, and open came the blouse and out came the breasts: big plump perfect white orbs with dark nipples as big around as the bottom of a beer bottle.

Morley nearly fell backwards at the delectable vision. He held out his hands in a pleading manner. "Could you please—"

"Shhh!" She pulled out a stool, plopped his ass down on it, and as abruptly as could be, sat on his lap. This action, of course, brought those bulbous, perfect tits right to his face. He sucked each nipple with adoration, drifting away in some lovely perfume scent on her skin. Her arms wrapped tight around him.

"Oh, my darling girl—," he began but she stopped him with another sharp "Shhh! Just be quiet, you, and *suck*," she whispered in his ear. Naturally Morley did as he was bid; all the while her hand fumbled at his crotch, feeling around down there, then unbuckling.

"My dear, I can give you five hundred reasons why you should—"

"Shhh! Damn!" She hopped off his lap, seeming adamant in some frenzied desperation. "I must see this cock Andela say so much of," she whispered, and in two deft yanks had his pants and shorts down to his knees. "She say eeze *perfect* cock and hard as piece of steel," and then she hastened to hoist her black work skirt and get her panties off.

Andela, Morley recollected. *Ah, yes, the maid who'd been sleeping in my closet earlier. So she's bragging about my penis to the other girls! What a wonderful woman!* "Did Andela really say that? That I have a perfect cock?"

"Shhh!" she whispered. "Yes!" and then she stepped back to look at it. Her eyes widened. "Ah, Bog! She eeze right! Eeze perfect!" and she'd pronounced *perfect* as *parfict.* She seemed to revere it, as one gazing upon a glittering holy relic. One hand cupped and squeezed the already constricting testicles, and the other squeezed his shaft rather hard, which pressured out a well of pre-ejaculant. "Andela is no lying! Eeze perfect and hard as a pipe! And it look almost too big to fit into me!"

Well, now, such comments as these were quite the ego booster for an overweight older man who'd never been in a genuine romantic relationship with a woman. Such circumstances were not Morley's style, and it was all a matter of commerce. To court a woman and then get married cost an enormous amount of money, yet for most men (if they were honest) the prime objective was sex. It was much easier and decidedly *cheaper* to solicit prostitutes. For a few hundred dollars he could get what he wanted and not have to bother with the abundance of things he *didn't* want. And of course most of these women he did hire commented that his penis was "huge," "giant," "a whopper," etc., but Morley was no fool. Naturally such women were going to lavish compliments upon the well-paying client; hence, the size of the tip. It was good business and common sense.

But the truth was Morley really had little else to compare his penis to. He'd never seen another man naked in person (nor did he want to!) and he rarely watched porn because it seemed to be an outright waste of time. Why "watch" when you had the money to "do?" Oh, back in his high school days, he'd measured it for posterity and found it to be just over nine inches erect, but he had no reason to believe this was anything more than average, because, after all, he was just an average man. His penis had brought him great pleasure in his life, but he really didn't care if it brought the women pleasure as well (after all, they were getting paid) but if it did, then that was all the nicer.

The barmaid didn't dawdle getting down to business. She manipulated herself up onto the stool, held up her skirt, and with a feverish look on her face, lowered her black-furred womanhood down over the entirety of his erection, all before Morley could even utter the slightest suggestion of condom-use. She moaned in a heated whispered, "Ahhhhhhhh—fock me! You have best cock of my life!"

This particular compliment sailed past Morley, whose face was pinking, eyes squeezed shut, as he tried to stave off the inevitable for as long a duration as possible. Meanwhile her hips slammed down on his lap over and over; she was impaling herself on his sexual goods. Then she leaned forward, shoved a nipple in his mouth and whispered, "Here! Again you suck this! Suck hard so milk come out. It feels good while focking."

"Milk?" Morley gasped.

"*Da*! I have baby none too long ago—"

Morley, of course, obliged her request and did indeed suck *hard*, until some warm, slightly sweet liquid came to his tongue, yet only then did her words actually register.

"Whuh? You said you had a baby?"

"*Da*, few months ago. Just suck!"

He had to exert himself to talk while in the rigors of intercourse. "Well, darling, I must say, if you don't stop and put a condom on me, you may well have *another* baby in nine months' time."

"Pah! I don't care! I want your jism in me, and if I have baby, *good!* I hope it be boy, so he have *your* big dick!"

Quite a conundrum, yes, but there was really nothing Morley could do. Women had proficient ways of rendering men powerless, and here was one such instance of that. He was past the point of no return, and evidently she was too. Her limbs stiffened around him as the stool rocked back and forth, and she was hissing whiny squeals through clenched teeth.

Morley's climax arrived as well. For a writer to describe such a thing really is a useless exercise in abstraction, so I will make no such endeavor, but I will tell you that it was a doozy. One big spurt after the next—*ten* of them, it seemed—were socked up into her vaginal barrel. It was an amount of semen that seemed completely undue—more like an eighteen year old's—but of course, Morley wasn't about to complain.

Next, the afterglow, if you could call it that in such a place as a cramped storage room in a bar. "Fock, you make me come like fockin' freight train," she said when she climbed off him (and quite wobbly she was); Morley had to brace himself so not to fall off the stool. He wobbled in place himself, trying to regain breath, and it was impossible not to notice a *slew* of semen running in a line down the inside of her leg.

Finally, when he could talk connectedly, he said, "What a wonderful, beautiful woman you are."

"*Da?* You think so?"

"Oh, yes, you are just the loveliest thing..."

But then the moment warped into the oddest stasis. The barmaid was just standing there, her stupendous bare tits still sticking out, and she was grinning at him, grinning in a way that was not at all pleasant.

"My dear, is...is something wrong?"

The silence held for a few seconds longer, and so did her vulturine grin. Here she whispered very slowly, "*Vracanje...*"

...a sting of pain pricked the left side of his neck, he flinched and uttered, "What in—" and then our Mr. Morley's world turned black.

Morley reports that some irreducible inkling of semi-consciousness fluttered in his mind amid the all-pervading blackness, and the nature of the experience unfolded as the most extreme collision of opposites that one could imagine.

In that blackness emerged glaring imagery both nauseating and abominable, companioned by ear-piercing shrieks and hideous screams; interwoven with this *horror* was a feeling of euphoria unlike anything he was capable of describing, other than saying it was the most wonderful, luxurious sensation permeating his entire being. This, of course, would be due to the high-grade morphine sulphate that had been injected into him.

Soon he was able to recollect, at least in part, that something very serious was underway. He struggled to make his brain work better within the euphoria, and then, in streams, he recalled what had happened in the storeroom of the bar: he'd been fucked silly by the barmaid, and then he'd been drugged. *Someone else was hiding in the room! It was a set up! She lured me back there just to drug me, and now...*

It was obvious, and rankly incontestible: Morley had been *abducted*. But to where?

The more he struggled against the drug's blissful and numbing rapture, the more he was able to cogitate the importance of regaining his senses. He had to grind his teeth in order to focus his smeared vision, and that's when he was able to logically examine his surroundings. He lay in some sort of metal compartment, but next he noticed a pair of closed doors, and to either side of him, wheel wells. The floor was corrugated metal. *Of course...* He was in the back of a windowless van.

A single dome light was all the light he had, a dim one at that. Naturally, the van's rear doors would be locked, but instinct ordered him to see for sure—however, the venture failed a moment later. The drug, it seemed, hadn't even come close to wearing off; Morley could barely move, much less crawl to the doors. But he was able, after a few grunts, to turn himself on his side because he'd just noticed what was there: his laptop.

Why would his abductors bring this from his room, unless... *There could be something on it they want me to see...*

It required a considerable effort, for his muscles felt like putty, but Morley strained himself and did manage to get his finger over to the laptop and press the power button, and as he did so he couldn't help but notice another SD card lying on the keyboard. The vivid screen buzzed to life, showing his nonchalant desktop. Picking the card up and inserting it into the slot took several tries due to his bloated coordination, yet eventually he succeeded. Morley lay in his buzzing stupor and watched the screen.

A nude woman had been staked to the ground in a forest, struggling against her bonds and evidently gagged for no screams could be heard, only muffled shrieks. Her face remained out of frame. It was a night scene, lit by portable lights on tripods. Several other women in black cloaks took turns standing over the naked victim, hoisting up their cloaks, and urinating in hard streams. Next it was a cloaked man who stepped between the captive's spread legs; he, too, hoisted his cloak, brandishing a prodigious erection, and he spat on the victim's sex, lay between her legs, and then vigorously fornicated with her for quite a length of time. The repeated impacts of his hips into her groin sounded like fists pounding raw meat. When he was finished, another cloaked man took his place, then another, then eight or ten more. When the last man had done, he rose and stepped away. Then the camera hovered in right close up to the woman's vagina, which had been pummeled so energetically that it had now swollen outward and looked like a bruised newborn baby's buttocks. A massive rill of soupy sperm issued slowly from the pounded orifice. The camera remained on this sight for a grueling amount of time.

Until now the only sounds detectable were the victim's gagged mewls, the rapid slapping of fornication, and an occasional crunching footstep over leaves. But at instant later, the entire scene on the screen *exploded* in an insane cacophony of sound: a power tool, not a chainsaw nor power drill but something which seemed even more nefarious. Now the camera rose and pulled aside, revealing as it swayed the dark confines of a forest clearing, several kerosene torches, and in between the shadows...*people*, people in black hooded cloaks peering forward. Then the source of the explosive machine sounds swayed into frame. Morley, even in his lethargic buzz, felt a jolt where he lay. The machine was a gas-powered roto-tiller, which wasted no time before dropping down into the staked woman's bare abdomen. The engine revved up as the tines bore down hard into the woman's soft guts, spraying blood and unwinding entrails in a demented abandon. Eventually the machine stopped.

Silence, save for a few *plips* of blood dripping from tree branches. And in a second, another of the cloaked men stepped right up, jerked up his cloak, and began fornicating with the eviscerated woman who was either dying or dead.

Now the camera edged away, at the onset of a grisly grinding sound; soon the sound's source became obvious. Even as the first man continued to sexually couple with the corpse, another man was kneeling, one hand opened on the victim's face and pressing down, and the other hand—

Morley vomited on the floor.

The other hand was cutting off the woman's head. It was with a largish coping saw sort of tool, and its amazingly thin blade ripped right through the tendons and muscle as if they were styrofoam, and with little more force it then ripped through the trachea and neckbone, and that was that.

The gush of blood looked black in the camera lights, and continued to well out with each new thrust of the man raping the corpse. But the affair on screen was not yet finished.

The head was lifted up and handed to another cloaked figure; the evidence of large braless breasts beneath the cloak made it plain the figure was a woman. She sat down Indian-style, cradling the head in her lap, and the peeled a length of duct tape off the victim's lips—

Morley's eyes bulged and he threw up again.

With this particular camera angle, the victim's face was easy to see in the light, and as the reader will likely have guessed by now, it was the head of Essie, his favorite girl in the whole world.

Morley felt as though he'd been dropped into some chittering maelstrom in hell, and could feel his mind reeling round and round in its revolting spiral. He lay inert, his cheek flat against the van's metal floor as he drooled and stared unblinking at the laptop screen.

A strange sound now whispered from the computer's speakers, something like *skritch, skritch, skritch...*, after which there followed an abysmally familiar activity. With the same foot-and-a-half-long carbon steel knife, the woman cradling Essie's staring head began to scrape off the skin from the face. For a moment, the bladeswoman paused and grinned right up into the camera. It was the hotel clerk, the woman who'd checked him in and looked a bit like Penelope Cruz.

Morley managed to close his eyes long enough to miss seeing Essie's entire scalp peeled off the top of her head, because in that short interlude, the camera had moved off again. It swept a full circle around the entire torch-lit scene. There seemed to be quite a few cloaked cultists (presumably they could be nothing else) standing within the skirt of shadows, their ghostly white faces looking on through the oval openings of their black hoods. The wavering torchlight made the scene seem almost medieval.

The camera broke from its slow sweep, then moved crookedly into the darker woods, footsteps crunching behind it. Here came another, smaller clearing, where a well-rotted corpse lay. Pretty much only bones remained, save for scraps of clothing around it: a shoulder-less summer dress evidently, though no vestige of its original color remained. Morley, even in his stupor, could guess that this was the pre-teen girl he'd seen murdered on the first SD card, whose production date had been a year ago. But then the camera zoomed in precisely on the skull, and Morley saw that it was covered with grayish-green moss, a small pinch of which was removed by the cameraman. Other footsteps approached—another cloaked figure, who placed Essie's now-completely-skinned head right next to the moss-covered skull.

My God, Morley managed the thought. *Poor Essie...* The total impact of the revelation would only strike him later: that *he* was no doubt the reason for her abominable murder, since these, these *people* had found her phone number on the paper card in Morley's pocket. That aside, the camera now homed in on Essie's severed head, which looked up in an open-eyed stare, with mouth agape. Fingers pushed the lower jaw down, to admit into the dead mouth a pair of pliers. The pliers, with a seeming expertise, clasped the tip of Essie's tongue and then pulled the tongue out of her mouth as far as it would go. Then—

snip!

About two inches of her tongue was cut clean off with a pair of tin snips.

The camera pulled back. Chuckles were heard. Two figures stepped up and hoisted up the cloak of the person who had snipped off the tongue, and in a moment it was plain that this person was a woman, for in the camera lights there now blared the image of the woman's pubic region, white skin contrasted sharply by a modest black pelt of fur.

The woman's fingers parted her cleft, and—perhaps with no surprise to the now-indoctrinated reader—used the severed tongue to ply up and down over her own clitoris. This act elicited a good many giggles from the other women present. After much theatrics with the tongue, the camera rose to show the giggling face of the woman who'd cut the tongue off: Andela, the girl he'd pitied when hearing of her employment travails. (At some later date, Morley discovered that the name *Andela* means *messenger* in Bosnian, and in some uses *messenger of the devil* or *messenger of death*.)

It was at this point that the SD card ended. The van doors banged open, men in cloaks lunged in, dragged him out, and that— quite mercifully—was all Morley remembered. All that followed was blacked out, manifestly, by the sheer trauma of it all…

And now, I hope the reader will not consider it a disservice or an ineptitude for me to truncate the remainder of events which affected my friend Mr. Morley so grievously. Much more did indeed happen to him before he was returned to the United States and his home in Florida, but I'm sorry to say that retelling those events via the expected manner of dramatized narrative is well beyond the limits of my nerves. It's just too ghastly.

Several weeks later he was able to return the U.S. (after a period of hospitalization), but not as anything close to the man he was, and of the abominable things that happened to him, fate was merciful enough to see to it that he remembered nothing more.

As best he could, he told me himself upon his return, with the events of his blackout left to obvious presumption. As you have surmised yourselves, for some reason he became the target of a close-knit conspiracy involving a group of—for lack of any other word— cultists, even satanists, and from there one might deduce that Morley was hexed via occult rites, modes of sacrifice, and even potions derived through secret arts. Ludicrous as this sounds, I believed every word of it the instant I saw him when he'd returned.

Right off, communication in person was nearly impossible, so he mostly had to resort to typing on a computer screen, after which I'd read what he'd written and then reply verbally. Why this? Because Morley's tongue had been cut off just like Essie's in the video, and we can fairly suspect what it was then used for. Thank God he didn't remember the actual act, nor did he remember the other barbarous acts perpetrated against him.

This wouldn't matter, though, because a few weeks after his return he received in his mailbox a small envelope with a postmark from Wroclaw, Poland. The return address was later found to be bogus.

This envelope contained an SD card, which understandably sent my friend into a state of terror. He absolutely refused to open the card on his computer, and advised me not to as well, but I pointed out that a close examination of the card might reveal some overlooked clue as to the actual identities of the perpetrators. Hence, Morley reluctantly agreed and waited in his living room while I commenced to watching the SD file in his office. This decision was the worst mistake of my life.

The card, of course, was a continuation of what happened that night in those eldritch woods, just as Morley was pulled from the van by a pack of cloaked figures. As we would all now expect, the leader of this coterie presented himself, the very man Morley first met upon entering the Iblis Hotel: the very short and physically defected "homeless bum" who'd demanded money. We know what happened then, and most everything after.

Morley was dragged to the nexus of this torch-lit clearing, was forced to his knees at knife point. The short man with foreshortened arm (we'll call him the leader from hereon), and in as few words as possible I will say that the little man stepped immediately out of his cloak and addressed Morley's face with his penis (which was disproportionately larger than one would expect to find on a man just over four feet tall) and then it was forced into Morley's mouth. Multiple knives at his throat, plus a nearby blow torch, were the perfect incentive for Morley *not* to bite. As he went through the act, however, Morley's distress became even more plain: he was gagging, hacking, tearing up, and at times looked as if he would vomit again, but then we will remember that this leader was a man who rarely washed (perhaps he never had) so his body odor was stupefyingly potent. Laughter circled about, and at one point it looked as if Morley would not be able to continue, but then the blow torch was lit, and Morley all too promptly returned to his ministrations of fellatio.

Next, one of the women of the sect knelt beside Morley. "No swallow, you must spit in this," she said, and just beneath his chin she held a large black bowl. In the background, dozens of cloaked figures had come forward to watch, and more than a few of them were fondling each other as they looked on over the "festivities." Finally the leader's hips bucked, he released a few guttural moans, and then he came in Morley's mouth. As instructed, he spat the sizable volume of sperm into the black bowl. It was here that Morley fell backward, heaving in fresh air in relief.

But no relief was forthcoming. Four men pinned Morley down, each by grabbing a limb. A fifth man sat down right on his chest, forced his mouth open with a crowbar, then another wielded pliers, yanked his tongue out, and—*snip!*—off it came.

Morley shouted blood. The tongue was held over the bowl, to drip blood into the semen, then it was tossed away. Morley was convulsing, his eyes starting from his head, and in an instant they were on him again. I'll keep this exposition as brief as possible.

They pulled down Morley's pants. They tied a leather string around the very base of his penis, and—

snip!

—the tin snips sheared it off in the space of an eye-blink.

A slow wave of the blow torch cauterized the wound (they obviously wanted their victim to live). Morley made sounds in reaction that were thoroughly inhuman. But even the least morbid of you will wonder what became of the penis after it was divorced from its host's body. Well...

Morley, now completely unconscious from shock, was flipped

over, his buttocks roughly spread, then a handful of Vaseline or some similar lubricant was slapped between them. Not only with a considerable finesse but a measure of expertise which denoted much practice, the limp flap of flesh that was once Morley's sex organ was thumbed right up into his anus. This action was promptly followed by the insertion of a large "butt-plug," so large, clearly, that it would take some doing for Morley to expel the penis of his own accord.

This account, I'm relieved to say, is nearly done.

Again, the black bowl was raised, along with a used condom that had been tied off once filled. Of course, this would be the same condom that Andela had put on Morley when she'd ravaged him. The condom was clipped, and its contents emptied into the bowl. Next, the short man—the leader—reappeared, back in his black raiments, pricked his thumb, and squeezed out several drops of blood into the bowl as well.

Now, mind you, the blood and sperm of two men were in the bowl, but before it could all be utilized for whatever sinister onus they'd so painstakingly planned, another ingredient first had to be added...

The cameraman's hand reached forward, then, and released into the bowl that small pinch of moss he'd plucked of the skull of the young girl who'd been debauched and murdered last year.

The bowl was put down on the ground, and at once the figure with the blow torch came forth. The torch was lit, and then the flame was lowered to the bowl. The contents of the bowl began to steam at once. It was carried off; the camera followed. Down a trail deeper into the woods, and then another clearing opened, and it was into this clearing that the entirety of this ominous membership emptied. A circle of smaller torches on sticks, perhaps twenty in all, comprised this circle, and before each torch there rested a skull—*ancient* skulls by the look of them. At the center of this illumined circle was placed a very naked, a very unconscious, and a very mutilated Mr. Morley.

The remainder of this "rite," and I suppose that is the correct word, was conducted by every cloaked member, one after another, dragging a finger inside the black bowl and then inscribing some illegible word on Morley's bare skin—each character, in other words, being written in the ashes of incinerated semen and blood. Amid the clearing there rose the sounds of half melodic chanting, in a language, of course, unknown to an American.

Another slow sweep of the camera highlighted the decrepit skulls before each torch, but beyond that I was able to detect, I think, even more skulls, all situated as if spectators to this undoubted exercise in diabolism. Within the lulling intonations of the chant, I believed I could repeatedly detect a word that sounded like "shaitan" or, alternately, "shayatin." (Later research would reveal—to no surprise—that these words were accepted substitutes in Islamic legendry for "Iblis"—the devil.)

After every member of the coterie had finger-scrawled a word or letter on Morley's still body, each and every one of them dropped their cloaks, selected a partner, and took to the torch-lit ground to partake in a bacchanal of the flesh the likes of which Caligula would approve. The activities will not be described.

This is where the video file ended.

Often, in tales of fiction (perhaps all *too* often), the endings are tied up neatly with all-too-convenient explanations. Not so in stories that are true, like this one.

We can only reasonably suspect that Mr. Morley, either due to random happenstance or something more deliberate, was targeted by a cult of transient Bosnians who were neither Christian nor Muslim but part of something quite antithetical to both. Ah, but we modern, educated persons do not give any credence to ideas like occultism.

Evidently, the wooded area where Mr. Morley met his near-death was tinctured by some dark history (this revealed by yours truly after some not-terribly-extensive research). Recall the long-regarded use of "potter's fields" throughout history (hearkening back to Biblical times) where the bodies of condemned criminals, suicides, miscreants, etc., were interred so as to keep them separated from the decedents of "good Christian folk."

Well, similar ideologies sprang up within the witch-cults of Europe dating back to before the Middle Ages but not necessarily involving "burial." Instead, there evolved quite a to-do about "corpse-relics" and "corpse-sorcery," wherein parts of dead bodies were considered extremely valuable; and in this particular arena the bones of the dead enjoyed a particular distinction. Bones of supposed witches and warlocks were exhumed with gusto by colleagues and aficionados, as the "broth" from such boiled bones was valuable in the preparation of all manner of potions, hex-balms, and diabolic philters. Likewise, these bones were also pulverized and spread on especial nights as fertilizer, so that what grew in such plots would prove useful to occultists.

Most interesting, however, was the demoniacal notion that skulls — the skulls of not the condemned nor the impious but of the innocent and the sacrificed — were highly regarded implements of the satanic practitioner. The skull would be skinned and flensed of all flesh, and then set down in the woods. After a year or so, moss and lichens would grow on said skull, and then be removed and used an ingredient for deviltry, witchery, and corpse-sorcery.

You may make such assumptions in this matter as you see fit, and though the evidence thus far is not very compelling on its own, there is one fact that I have not as yet mentioned.

Upon Mr. Morley's return to the United States, it is true that he had been left genitally mutilated and tongueless. He was, at that time, otherwise the same stoutish man of nearly six feet in height that I had always known.

However, after the lapse of several months, he was no longer that … but instead a very lean man who was barely over four feet tall and whose arms had grievously shriveled to the length of about a foot.

THE STATEMENT OF SGT. JESSOP

THE STATEMENT OF SGT. JUSTIN JESSOP OF THE INNSMOUTH POLICE DEPARTMENT

INTERVIEWER: When did you realize that something was seriously wrong?

JESSOP: Yesterday morning about 8 a.m. I was in the patrol car, so the chief radioed me and said that Hanna Tilton just called, said a man with no legs was dragging himself across the New Church Green. We both kind of laughed at that, 'cos Hanna Tilton's about ninety and nuttier than a truckload of fruitcakes. Hell, last Christmas she called and said Santa Claus had come down her chimney—with his dick out—and Hanna doesn't even *have* a chimney. Anyway, I had to check it out, so I drove the car over and...and—

INTERVIEWER: What did you find?

JESSOP (sighs): I found Matt Eliot dragging himself across the Green with no legs. I got out and tried to help him but there wasn't anything I could do. His legs looked ripped out of his hip sockets, no stumps to get tourniquets on. Whoever did it also pulled his cock and balls off and put it in his shirt pocket. No lie. What kind of lunatic would do something like that? Anyway, right before he died he said, "Tis all true, Justin. The stories from the old days. Them things started comin' ashore from the reef about sun up, bust right into the plant where we was all workin'—"

INTERVIEWER: The *plant?* Can you specify?

JESSOP: On Water Street. Matt works in one of the fish-packing plants there...or I should say *worked.* "They kicked all the loading doors down," he said. "Barged right in and start killin' everyone, pullin' off heads, yankin' out guts. Throwed Ezra Dunning, the floor super, right smack dab into the chum-chopper. And any women workin' the gutting line—well, those things got right to it, fuckin' them gals every which way while's they was screamin' to high heaven. The prettier ones, like Marsha Cobb'n Belinda Bishop—they carried 'em off, and the old ones'n not so good lookin' ones, shit, they fed 'em right through the big band saw we use to cut up the tunas. Ya could tell by lookin' at 'em—they was doin' it just fer *fun...*" That's when Matt bled out, so first thing I did was get on the radio but before I could call for backup, Chief Dodgeson was on the line, screaming: "Jessop! Get out'a town! These things come up Madison street and are all over the place, killin' everybody!" and then came some gunshots, some grisly tearing sounds and—that was the last I heard from the chief.

INTERVIEWER: So, what were the "things?" Did you see them yourself?

JESSOP: "For shit's sake! Of course I saw 'em, then, and after they died! You're telling me that you didn't see the bodies?

INTERVIEWER: This isn't about what *I* saw, sergeant. Let's keep this interview objective. It's about what you saw.

JESSOP: Well, fuck, okay. The things mostly looked like what the old Innsmouth legends say: big watery eyes that never blink;

long, thin-lipped mouths; creases of skin on the sides of their necks that look like they might be gills. Bunch of fucked-up deformities all mixed up to one degree or another with human aspects.

INTERVIEWER: Would you describe the non-human traits as ichthyic or batrachian?

JESSOP: The *fuck?* What's that mean?

INTERVIEWER: Fish-like, frog-like, that sort of thing?

JESSOP: Yes, yes—whatever! Worse than that! Most of 'em had fully changed over—you know, like the legend says, and some of 'em—fuck!—they must've been the full-blooded ones, like the old stories talk about. Then I drove down past the fire station—jeez! The fuckin' place was on fire! And there was something wrong with the radio—I couldn't get through anywhere, not even on the state band. Cellphone wouldn't work either, almost like those things had some way to jam it. So then I tear-ass over to the Holiday Inn Express that used to be the old Gilman House Hotel, thought I could use their landline but, fuck... First thing I see when I went in was three of these things all fuckin' the front desk girl at the same time, one gettin' her in the ass, the other in the—you know—her cooch, and the other had pulled her fuckin' *head* off and was fuckin' her, her neck-hole, you know? Her esophagus I guess, and damned if there wasn't a fourth one tryin' to jerk off in the severed head's mouth. And don't ask me to describe the dicks on these things 'cos I won't. But when they see me standin' there, they all stop and start to come after me, so I dropped the lot of 'em with four single head-shots. I notice through the front window that a bunch of others already had my patrol car tipped over and were setting it on fire, and the worst part was they tipped it over deliberate on Brandy Babcock from the bakery, who was eight months pregnant, and then I see more of 'em pourin' into the town square and coming out of the rec center that they say used to be that weirdo church, Something-or-other Order of the Dragon or Dagon or something like that. I just said fuck it and ran out the hotel's back door. Even with all the screaming coming from the rooms, there wasn't anything I could do. I hauled ass across Lafayette Street, cut through the old Marsh lot where that mansion used to be, then found myself in the back way of the old closed church on Adam's Lane. I jimmied my way in and finally found the stairs to the bell tower, so that's where I went, right up those stairs into the tower. I peeked down from the tower, took one look toward the docks, and passed out.

INTERVIEWER: What did you see?

JESSOP: What do ya think? More of those things, but not hundreds of 'em, *thousands* of 'em, *thousands* of those, of those *monsters*. When I saw all that, I guess I went into shock and lost consciousness. Didn't wake up again for almost twenty-four hours, and that's when I came down 'cos I saw the military vehicles and all those front loaders shoveling up all the bodies of those things.

INTERVIEWER: You're a very lucky man, Sergeant Jessop. Only a few other townspeople survived.

JESSOP: Well...how did you kill them all like that? At first I thought it might be something like nerve gas or something, but then I would've died too, right?

INTERVIEWER: It wasn't us, sergeant. You really want to know what killed all those things? Well, I'll tell you. It was the fucking coronavirus...

END

ABOUT THE AUTHOR

Edward Lee is an American novelist specializing in the field of horror, and has authored over 50 books. Lee is particularly known for over-the-top occult concepts and an accelerated treatment of erotic and/or morbid sexual imagery and visceral violence.

www.ingramcontent.com/pod-product-compliance
Lightning Source LLC
Chambersburg PA
CBHW051119260626
47170CB00005B/1576

* 9 7 8 1 6 2 1 0 5 3 2 5 5 *